the further adventures of
SHERLOCK HOLMES

THE DEVIL'S PROMISE

THE DEVIL'S PROMISE

DAVID STUART DAVIES

WITH A FOREWORD BY MARK GATISS

TITAN BOOKS

THE FURTHER ADVENTURES OF SHERLOCK HOLMES:
THE DEVIL'S PROMISE
Print edition ISBN: 9781783292707
E-book edition ISBN: 9781783292714

Published by Titan Books
A division of Titan Publishing Group Ltd
144 Southwark Street, London SE1 0UP

First edition: November 2014
10 9 8 7 6 5 4 3 2 1

A CIP catalogue record for this title is available from the British Library.

Printed in the USA.

What did you think of this book? We love to hear from our readers.
Please email us at: readerfeedback@titanemail.com,
or write to Reader Feedback at the above address.

To receive advance information, news, competitions, and exclusive offers online,
please sign up for the Titan newsletter on our website:
www.titanbooks.com

To William Gillette, Eille Norwood, Arthur Wontner, Basil Rathbone, Peter Cushing, Douglas Wilmer, Christopher Plummer, Jeremy Brett and Benedict Cumberbatch, all of whom have brought the character of Sherlock Holmes to dramatic life.

Foreword

SOME THOUGHTS ON SHERLOCK HOLMES

I am writing this in a break in the filming of *Sherlock*, the BBC series in which I am heavily involved as writer, actor and co-creator. Sherlock Holmes has been a life-long obsession of mine and it is a dream come true to be presenting our two favourite characters from Baker Street on screen. Sherlock Holmes has always meant the world to me. I first discovered him through the Basil Rathbone films and *The Adventures of Sherlock Holmes* – the first book I bought about the Great Detective. I vividly remember Eric Ambler's introduction to that volume which ends with him saying, 'I wish I were reading these stories for the first time.' I remember thinking, 'Oh, I am.' And I was over the moon.

I think that Sherlock Holmes is imperishable, a brilliant British icon – indeed a worldwide icon. He represents the best of us. He is as clever as we would all like to be. He is surprising, capricious, slightly dangerous, strangely elegant, dashing, Byronic and the best and wisest man any of us will ever know.

I believe he lasts because we all want to be Sherlock Holmes and we all want to believe there are people like Sherlock Holmes out there, instead of the universe being completely chaotic, which is actually the truth.

This fabulous character is the creation of Arthur Conan Doyle who, in my opinion, was a writer of genius. No wonder so many of us wish to tread in his footsteps. Sherlock now lives in other people's stories, too, as he does in *The Devil's Promise*, penned by the great Davies, whose Sherlock Holmes writings have brought me hours of pleasure.

Mark Gatiss

During the 1880s the name Bartholomew Blackwood was infamous in Britain. He was known as 'The Devil's Companion'. Blackwood, a self-proclaimed disciple of Satan, was vilified by the press and public alike as being the embodiment of evil.

He was the only son of a rich brewer from the Midlands and as a child he had been pampered and spoilt by his doting parents. Their misguided indulgence robbed the boy of many of the more sensitive feelings towards his fellow man. He grew into an arrogant and selfish youth. At university he studied languages and philosophy in a desultory fashion, gaining only a third class degree. However, he developed a strong interest in religion and on graduation he became determined to enter the ministry. Despite protestations from his ailing father, who wanted his son to take the helm of the brewery firm, Bartholomew Blackwood became ordained into the Christian church.

Blackwood very quickly renounced the teachings of Jesus and became a follower of the seventeenth-century Italian demonologist Francesco Maria Guazzo, whose writings included his infamous magical pact with the Devil, the ceremony of Corpus Diablo. Based on Guazzo's grimoires, Blackwood initiated his own satanic cult, The Fellowship of the Dark Dawn, and using money from his inheritance, he purchased Stokely Abbey in the Fen country to provide a haven for his followers. Here they studied, researched and developed their abominable creed. The horrified public heard wild tales concerning the activities at the abbey – stories of drugs, debauchery and obscene ceremonial rites, some including human sacrifice. It was recorded that Blackwood believed that all such abominations were leading him closer to his ultimate goal: a union between himself and the Devil. Eventually a vigilante group of locals set fire to the place, believing that the conflagration would cleanse the countryside of its foul infection. Many members of the Order perished in the flames, but Blackwood managed to escape, although he was badly scarred. He fled to France with his 'wife' Elenora where she gave birth to twins. For some fifteen years Blackwood stayed in France, where he continued to study and research the occult. He tried to publish his numerous tracts but no publisher would touch them, branding them blasphemous and obscene.

Blackwood remained obsessed with the idea of carrying out the ceremony of Corpus Diablo, which would bring about that most terrible of goals: a corporeal manifestation of the Devil himself. Some claim that he did succeed and that the experience drove him mad. Not long before his death, his mind tormented with insane thoughts and his feeble body worn out by drink, drugs and general excess, Blackwood was secretly brought back to England by the rich followers of the Fellowship in order that he could die in his own country. Once on British soil, he seemed to disappear. There were unconfirmed reports of him living in Scotland and in Yorkshire, but no one knew for sure and there was no official record of his death. But by now a new century was about to dawn and the public had lost interest in this strange old man. There were new sensations to occupy the pages of the popular press.

Strangely no one ever enquired after his children, the offspring of one of the most evil men that ever lived – the man the press had called The Devil's Companion.

What follows is a remarkable tale of events which took place in the year 1899 and concern the involvement of both Sherlock Holmes and John H. Watson in their darkest and most remarkable adventure. I have spent many years researching this brilliant detective whom Watson regarded as 'the best and wisest man whom I have ever known'. Researches in Britain, Switzerland and America have brought me into contact with many rare documents pertaining to Holmes and Watson's career. Gradually, I have been able to build up the complete story of what happened in those fateful months on the cusp of the twentieth century. Now at last I am able to place before the public the full narrative, and chilling denouement of this terrible story.

David Stuart Davies

Part One

From Dr Watson's Journal

I found Sherlock Holmes on the beach. He was perched like some great dark bird of prey on a large rock gazing out to sea. On the farther horizon, the morning sun rose above the grey, rolling swell, sending dazzling splinters of orange light across the water. Holmes was apparently oblivious to my approach; his stern hawk-like features, bleached by the dawn light, indicated that he was deep in thought. However, as I reached his side, he spoke to me without averting his gaze from the sea.

'Been doing some detective work of your own, Watson?'

'More like instinct, I'm afraid. When I came down for breakfast and observed that you'd gone out, I knew where you would be. I believe even Lestrade could have worked that one out.'

Holmes gave a harsh laugh and his features lightened for a moment. 'I suspect you are right.' He fumbled in the pocket of his overcoat and withdrew a cigarette case and a box of matches. 'Care to join me?' he asked after lighting a cigarette, caving his hands around the match to protect the meagre flame from the wind.

I shook my head.

For some moments we remained silent, watching the dun-coloured breakers surrender their force onto the beach while at the far end of the bay waves smashed against the steep rugged rocks with fragmented white foam.

'How far we seem now, Watson,' my friend said at last, 'from handmade London. From those artificial boundaries which we create to keep nature at bay. It is so easy to forget the monumental power of the natural world while encased in that city. Being here with the wind and the waves and the sky – such a large sky unfettered by spires and rooftops – one is reminded how small we are, how futile our gestures are as we strut and posture along the path of life. Long after you and I are but grains of dust in some rotting graveyard, this beach, that sky and those waves will still be here.'

'A melancholy thought.'

'Only because sentiment makes it so. I am glad, old fellow, that you persuaded me to take this holiday. It has allowed me time to think – to really think. There have been no clients, no interruptions and no other intellectual distractions to divert my thoughts.'

'Where have they led you?'

Holmes shrugged. 'I'm not sure. I am still pondering…' He paused and took a long pull on his cigarette.

'Ah, well, I gathered that,' said I. 'It was the nature of your thoughts that puzzled me.'

'I think the time is coming for me to give up my detective practice and retire.'

I smiled. 'I believed that you might say that.'

Holmes raised an eyebrow. 'How perspicacious.' A ghost of a smile trembled momentarily on his lips.

'It is understandable. There have been no stimulating cases for you of late and it has left you time to ruminate, to contemplate and measure the grains of your life. Times passes apace. We are about to enter a new century. In a few years I will be fifty. A time when most men contemplate shrugging off the shackles of work and responsibility in exchange for quiet days and early bedtimes…'

The gaunt grey face relaxed into a smile once more. 'Your years with me have not been wasted. You have seen and you have observed.'

'But you are not most men. And to turn your back on the pursuit and the detection of crime in order that you can retire…'

'And study bees. I have often thought I would like to study bees. I admire their industry, their organisation, and their dedication to the task in hand.'

'Stop it, Holmes,' I cried with some passion. 'Stop it now. You must not surrender to this malaise. Fight it as you fought Moriarty on the edge of the Reichenbach Falls. You are the man you have always been. Age will not wither you…'

'Ah, you add Shakespeare to your potent mix of persuasion. Spare me the poetry.' His hooded eyes flashed darkly and he rose, flicking the half-smoked cigarette into the sand and faced me, his features troubled and stern. 'You mean well, Watson. You always mean well and I've shamefully used and abused your goodness in the past. The trouble is that you care for me and therefore your judgement is useless. Where is the objective thinking in the bleatings of a loving friend? I can only answer, as I always do, to my brain, to my intellectual processes, which are sympathetic to no man. *They* will guide me, be my lodestar. Not you, my dear Watson.'

So saying, Holmes turned and walked away, towards the water's edge. Not for the first time, his words had hurt me, but I took small consolation in the fact that they were not meant to. Holmes believed that truth was pure and it must be embraced, however painful it was to others as well as to himself.

I gazed after him, now a slim shimmering silhouette framed by the rising sun, staring out to sea, his shoulders sunk into the great folds of his coat, and for the first time since I had known Sherlock Holmes, I felt sorry for him.

It had needed all my powers of persuasion to coax my friend into taking this holiday on the Devonshire coast. He had been in a black mood for some time and I knew that unless he was shaken out of it, he would sink further down into that perennial pit of despond that awaited him when spirits were low. But somehow, this time, the situation was far worse.

With all brilliant minds, the balance that controls the mental equilibrium is easily upset. A spring which was almost devoid of interesting cases to engage his mind had been followed in early June by the news that his brother Mycroft had suffered a stroke. For some days Mycroft hovered on the edge of death but his inner reserve pulled him back from the brink. He made a reasonable recovery but was now confined to a wheelchair, a fate that had increased his irritability. For Holmes the experience was a salutary one. Although he had dealt with death many times in his investigations, it had been in the business of detective work. Mycroft's brush with the grim reaper had encroached on my friend's sensibilities. Its effect was twofold. He had realised how much he really cared for his corpulent brother and he was also reminded of his own fragile mortality. Usually Holmes' mind was so channelled into specific passions – whether it be tracing the motets of Lassus or writing a monograph on some arcane aspect of criminal detection – that he never contemplated the fact that the grains of sand were slipping, irrevocably, through the narrow channel of life's hourglass and filling up the lower chamber.

In the old days, I would have said that all Holmes needed was a puzzling case to shake him from the malaise that enshrouded him when days were dull and there was no call upon him to exercise his detective skills. But I realised that something more radical was needed now. I thought that if I could lure him away from the familiar locales of London for a while to allow him to refresh his mind in new surroundings, this would be the start to the healing process. To be honest, I was hoping that some solution to my dilemma might occur to me as we took our cliff top walks and breathed in the cleansing sea air.

At this time I had returned to my old lodgings in Baker Street while my wife was visiting her sick sister in America, a trip that was likely to take six to nine months. I did not relish the prospect of living alone in her absence and I also believed that my presence at 221B might well help revitalise Holmes and return him to his old self. However, after only a few weeks of residence there, I could see that it would take more than the presence of an old fellow lodger to raise his spirits. Something else must be done.

I learned of Samphire Cottage near the village of Howden in Devon from Cawthorne, one of my new cronies at the billiard club. He had taken his wife there to recuperate after a major operation and apparently the isolated environment and clean air had revived not only her health but her spirits also. Here seemed the ideal prescription for my friend. A few weeks away from the grime of London and the overly familiar environments, which were now suffocating Holmes' spirit, might well work its magic on him, too. Of course, the problem was to convince my friend of the benefit of such a vacation.

After much cajoling and persuasion, along with the help of our housekeeper Mrs Hudson who, in her canny way, had also noted a change in her lodger's demeanour, I succeeded. Eventually I wrought an agreement from Sherlock Holmes that he would join me at the cottage for one week – 'and one week only, Watson.'

It was a start.

And so on a bright July afternoon we came to the little whitewashed dwelling which sat on the edge of the cliffs like a great brooding gull. We had travelled by train to Totnes and then hired a small carriage to drive the rest of the way and to be our conveyance for the duration of the stay. That had been two days prior to our conversation on the beach.

On arriving, we quickly settled our domestic arrangements and although Holmes was more than usually quiet, he was congenial. For most of the time he took himself off on solitary walks carrying a spyglass which he had discovered in one of the cupboards in the cottage or he sat before the fire, his long legs tucked under him, scribbling footnotes in red ink in a large copy of *The Pilgrim's Progress* that he had brought with him.

I have always considered myself a patient man and I knew that it would take time to unravel that knot which held the real character of my friend in its thrall. Frustrating though it was to see him like this, I knew I could and indeed would wait.

I rose and stretched, still not feeling fully awake. By now Holmes had disappeared behind a large outcrop of rock near the water's edge and the beach was deserted. The gulls wheeled high above me, their shrill harsh cries heard above the roar of the surf. I was about to turn and make my way back to the cottage when suddenly there was another sound to join this cacophony. It was Holmes' voice. He had reappeared from behind the line of rocks and was running towards me with his hands held before him as though in an act of supplication.

'Watson, for God's sake…'

I took a few faltering steps towards him and then stopped dead. I saw that the hands of Sherlock Holmes were dripping with blood.

Two

From Dr Watson's Journal

'Come, man, come,' cried Sherlock Holmes, his eyes more alive than I'd seen them in many a long day. His body turned awkwardly, ready to retrace his steps, but he waited for me to respond.

'What is it, Holmes?' I cried, my eyes fixed on his upraised palms, glistening red in the early morning sun.

'Unless my faculties have failed me altogether, it is murder, my friend, brutal murder.'

I shook my head in some confusion.

'A body,' he said. 'Beyond the rocks. Come.'

He turned and I followed. We set off at a brisk pace, our feet sinking into the moist sand.

'I thought it was a large piece of driftwood at first,' cried Holmes, over his shoulder, 'but when I reached it…'

Together we clambered over the rocks, Holmes ahead of me, eagerly negotiating his way across the slippery terrain.

'It wasn't driftwood,' he continued. 'It was the body of a man. A middle-aged man – somewhere in his late fifties, I should say.'

'He has been washed ashore?'

Holmes shook his head. 'No, no. His clothes were dry. And he couldn't have fallen from the cliff top – his body lay too far from the base. Besides there were severe wounds to his head indicating that he had been attacked from behind.'

'Surely he could have sustained such wounds by falling from the cliff.'

'Possibly, but he would have received other injuries also. To the face, for instance. And his clothes would have been torn. But this was not the case.'

'You think that he was murdered on the beach?' I could hardly believe the circumstances my friend was describing.

'No, I don't think that.'

By now we had traversed the outcrop of rocks and reached the new area of beach.

'Where is this body?' I asked, scanning the empty shoreline.

Holmes stopped in his tracks, his eyes wide with surprise. 'It was… it was there,' he said, indicating a bare patch of sand. 'But it has gone.'

'Gone!' I exclaimed. 'But that's impossible.'

Holmes pointed a finger at me. 'No, Watson, not impossible. Improbable, I grant you, but the two are not the same. Only a fool dismisses the improbable.'

'You say there was a dead body here and now it has gone.'

'I do,' snapped Holmes, lifting his eyes to scan the cliff top behind us. There was nothing or no one to be seen. 'Obviously the body had been left on the beach to be carried out to sea. It is likely the murderers were in the process of dragging it to the water's edge when they spied me clambering over the rocks and so they dropped it and ran for cover.'

'Murderers. You think that there was more than one?'

'Yes, yes, of course,' he snapped impatiently, his eyes flashing with suppressed frustration. 'One man could not have brought a body down here from the cliff top on his own. There must have been at least two of them.'

'What body?' I asked with some incredulity, viewing the empty beach.

Holmes narrowed his eyes, glaring at me for a moment, and then, suddenly, his thin lips broke into a tight smile. 'Ah, so now you add madness to my melancholia. The old boy has begun hallucinating. There are no murders on hand to investigate, so in desperation I conjure one up out of thin air. Is that it?'

I knew that hallucinations were not unusual in cases of deep depression but I had not considered that such an emotional reaction could affect my friend. But his own mention of such a possibility sent out danger signals.

I shook my head reassuringly. 'Look, Holmes, of course I believe you… but who else will? Where is the body? Where are the signs that there was a body?'

He held up his fingers caked with dried blood. 'Fresh from the wound at the back of the head…'

'Then surely there will be traces of blood on the sand.'

'Possibly,' commented Holmes, tersely, but without conviction.

'And footprints,' I added.

'They could have easily been smoothed away,' he murmured.

In silence we searched the area in vain. There were no crimson spots or smears on the virgin beach and no imprint to suggest a body had lain there.

'How do you explain it, Holmes?'

He shook his head. 'I can't. I can't. The culprits could have hidden behind that sand dune yonder on hearing my approach. They would not have had time to struggle with the body, so they left it and, concealing themselves, watched me. As soon as I ran off to you… they scooped up the cadaver…'

'Yes...?'

'Ah, well, that's where my deductions run out. Too little data.'

'Well, at least we can take a look behind the sand dune for signs.'

'There will be none – but nevertheless we may as well look.'

Holmes was correct. There were no footprints or any other signs to indicate that two men had been standing there. And again there was no blood.

'Why were you so sure that we'd find nothing when you believe the murderers were here?' I asked.

'Clever men. Too clever to be caught that way,' Holmes cried, dabbling his fingers in a shallow pool to wash the blood from them.

'Tell me more about the corpse. You say he was middle-aged. How was he dressed?'

'A white shirt, coarse quality material, dark trousers. Anonymous clothing I'm afraid. He had only one shoe. He had a pale complexion and his nose was marked by indentations at the bridge suggesting that he wore spectacles. His hands were soft and without the telltale marks of manual labour. No rings or other obvious markings that I could see.'

'Well, I am puzzled, Holmes.'

'It is one of those rare occasions when we share that same emotion, Watson.' Holmes gave a short braying laugh. 'I can imagine you writing this up in the *Strand* as "The Unsolved Case of the Disappearing Corpse".'

I gave a weak smile and said nothing. But what I wanted to say was: 'Holmes, there *is* no case. All I have is your word that you found a corpse on the beach. There is no indication that such a thing existed. And you have just washed away any evidence to corroborate your story in a beach pool. For all I know, that substance on your hands could well have been red ink, the red ink you have been using for your notes back at the cottage. In your current state of mind, I could quite believe that you did indeed manufacture this little drama as some kind of escape from the pit of despair into which you have fallen.'

Holmes turned to me and gave me a brief nod, his eyes flashing wildly, indicating that he knew what I was thinking.

And so we stood like uncertain statues on that deserted beach, the sound of the wind and the waves pounding in our ears, both at a loss what to say or what to do. I felt adrift from my friend. In all the years I'd known him and in all the strange and exotic humours he had exhibited, I always knew, often instinctively, how to act in order to defuse a dangerous situation or develop an uncertain one.

But not now.

Without warning Holmes crouched down and picked up a handful of sand and let it filter through his fingers. 'O, what a noble mind is here o'erthrown.'

'Holmes… I…'

'I crave a little sustenance and a warm fire. I believe I am ready to continue my studies again.'

I nodded and solemnly we made our way back to the cottage.

Three

❦

From Dr Watson's Journal

After an early lunch, Holmes wrapped himself in a travelling rug by the fire with the copy of *The Pilgrim's Progress* and continued his note making. No more was said about the supposed corpse on the beach and I felt reluctant to raise the subject. I really did not know what to make of the matter. Instead, I tried to lose myself in a hefty seafaring novel that I had brought with me, but constantly my mind was pulled away from mountainous waves, creaking timbers and ferocious seadogs to dwell on the mental state of my old and dearest friend. In the end I tossed the book to one side and picked up the latest copy of *The Lancet*. I knew that where Holmes' condition was concerned my medical knowledge was limited. It would need a more informed medical mind than mine to return him to his old self. I realised that I would by some means have to persuade him to see a specialist in mental disorders. Someone who could unlock the chained repressions that were holding Holmes prisoner. It was then that an article on psychoanalysis caught my eye.

As evening drew its darkened wings around the cottage, Holmes thrust his work aside and sank even lower in the chair. He spoke for the first time since lunch. 'I must tell you that I have no inclination to visit Vienna, Watson,' he observed with a nod to my reading matter before closing his eyes.

After the moment of initial surprise, a smile spread across my face. The old devil!

I woke early the next morning with a sudden start. A sharp, steely thought had thrust its way through the veil of sleep and prompted me into consciousness. I rubbed my eyes as the thought nagged at me: what if I had been wrong and there had been a body on the beach? Was it possible that I was allowing my feelings about Holmes' condition to mask what may be the truth? His comment of the previous evening – the reference to Vienna – indicated that his detective skills were still as sharp as ever. He had read my thoughts and determined that I was thinking of Sigmund Freud, who practised in that city. He had deduced that I had come across the article on Freud in *The Lancet* and, aware of my concern for his erratic behaviour, he had cleverly made the connection without any prompting comment from me. This casual demonstration clearly revealed that despite his malaise, his professional skills were not lying dormant.

I leapt from my bed and within twenty minutes I'd had a quick wash, dressed and was hurrying from the cottage. Before leaving, I opened the door of my friend's bedroom a fraction to make sure that he was asleep. My effort was rewarded by the sound of the regular heavy breathing that denotes deep slumber. I guessed that he would not be awake for another hour at least.

Rather than take my usual route down to the shore – a track some quarter of a mile from the cottage – I walked further along the cliff top in search of another way down to the beach, nearer to the spot where Holmes claimed to have seen the body. Sure enough there was another path half a mile further along. It was neglected and overgrown and somewhat tortuous but nevertheless I gauged that it was negotiable. Before attempting the trek down to the distant shore, I scrutinised the terrain around about to see if I could find any signs of recent visitors. To my delight I discovered distinct tracks in the soft sandy earth near the pathway. They were tracks of a horse-drawn carriage or cart: solid wheels had imprinted themselves clearly and other impressions suggested that the conveyance had been drawn by one heavily hoofed horse with a misshapen shoe on its off foreleg. Of course this discovery did not verify Holmes' story but it certainly presented evidence to support it.

Buoyed up by this knowledge, I made my way down the rough pathway, my eyes searching for other signs of recent passage and, in particular, signs of blood. I saw none. The absence of blood seemed to me to be a great stumbling block. If, as Holmes described, the body was bleeding from savage wounds to the skull, there were bound to be splashes of blood somewhere. If not on the path or nearby foliage, then on the beach near to where the body had been laid. And, as I had ascertained the previous day, there were none. One thing I did espy however was a brass buckle lodged in a tuft of grass. Examining it, I decided that this could possibly have come from the man's shoe. Holmes said that the corpse was only wearing one shoe. Whether the buckle was of any significance I knew not but I pocketed it just in case.

The beach itself was now a blank canvas. The tide had had its way with it, creating a set of new bland ribbed patterns in the sand. Any bloodstains would have been washed away. And besides I had been there the previous day and seen none. I gazed around me, a despondent cloud settling about my enthusiasm once more, and then... then I saw it. Some distance away beneath the overhang of a grass-tufted dune was something that looked like the legs of a large albino spider poking from the wet sand, but as I approached I could see quite clearly that they were in fact fingers – human fingers reaching out from their yellow prison.

I dropped to my knees and scooped the sand away in a desperate attempt to expose more of what my fearful heart believed was a dead body. Before long I had revealed the hand and the arm of the corpse – for indeed that is what it was. The arm was rigid: rigor mortis had been set in for some time. Holmes had been right all along – my brain thundered with the thought. How had I dared to doubt him?

With my bare hands I dug furiously, gradually revealing more of the entombed corpse. In time, I cleared away the sand from the head. Dragging a handkerchief from my coat pocket, I gently dusted the last damp grains away from the dead man's face. The features were just as Holmes had described them, down to the indentations either side of the nose that indicated that the man had been a regular wearer of spectacles or a pince-nez. I sat back on my haunches and despite the coolness of the morning, sweat dripped from my brow. Now what was I to do? It was pointless digging the body completely out of the sand on my own. It would be impossible for me to move it single-handed and yet I couldn't very well leave it here, exposed as it was, in case some other early morning stroller came upon it.

Reluctantly, I covered up the body again with a thin layer of sand so that it was hidden once more and marked the spot with a piece of driftwood lying nearby. And then I scrambled back up the path, my heart pounding and my senses strangely elated, and made my way back to the cottage.

Four

From Dr Watson's Journal

I raced back to the cottage, my mind awhirl with possibilities. I burst through the door that led immediately into the cosy sitting room to discover Sherlock Holmes in conversation with a stranger. He was a tall, muscular man dressed in black with a clerical collar. He was leaning forward in his seat clutching a cup of tea, his earnest features set in mid-discourse. Both men turned suddenly and silently at my abrupt entrance.

'Ah, Watson, back from your constitutional,' said Holmes cheerily.

I nodded dumbly.

Our visitor rose and extended his hand.

'I am so very pleased to meet you, sir,' he said pleasantly, and added, 'The Reverend Simon Dickens at your service.'

I mumbled my own name as we shook hands but it was clear that this stranger knew who I was. I sloughed off my overcoat and joined the two men by the recently lit fire which, as yet, was struggling to make its warmth felt.

'As I explained to Mr Holmes,' said our visitor, resuming his seat,

'I am the vicar of Howden – a hamlet some three miles north of here – and while rambling along the cliff top – as is my wont in the early morning – I noticed smoke emerging from your chimney. As the cottage has been uninhabited for some time I thought I'd better... introduce myself to the new parishioner, as it were.'

'Or check that no unlawful entry had been perpetrated,' Holmes added dryly.

The cleric smiled. 'I suppose that was part of my thinking also. Isolated dwellings so easily become the prey of the criminal fraternity. Just because here in the country we are far removed from the evils of the great cities does not mean that we are without our fair share of ne'er-do-wells.'

'I am pleased to hear it,' said Holmes, mischievously. 'I am a detective after all and crime is my bread and butter.'

Our visitor seemed somewhat nonplussed at this observation but Holmes carried on blithely. 'However, as I was about to explain before my friend burst in upon us so robustly' – a nod in my direction – 'we can hardly be regarded as parishioners. Our tenancy here is temporary and concludes at the end of the week.'

Simon Dickens nodded. 'How disappointing. It would be rather splendid if someone as notable as yourself were part of our community. Your good deeds are well known, even in this rural backwater, thanks of course to your splendid narratives, Doctor Watson.' He extended his arm in my direction.

I smiled in response. My heart rate was only just returning to normal after my exertions.

'Despite what you may have heard or read, I am sure that neither Watson, nor I – especially myself – would be ideal parishioners, Reverend. I have never been a particularly God-fearing man. As someone who has based his life and career on the pursuit of logic and rationality, religion has always been a suspect area for me. Much of what we are asked to believe has to be taken on trust without any significant supporting evidence.'

Simon Dickens gave my friend an indulgent smile. 'So much of life is like that, Mr Holmes. We have to trust that the moon comes out tonight and that the sun will rise tomorrow and indeed that the rain will water the crops. There is no certainty – only our trust.'

'Ah,' said Holmes, warming to the debate, 'but as our colleagues in the legal profession would point out, the incidence of regularity – moon rising, sun rising, rain falling – is based on precedence. Just as the tide comes in and then recedes. We have seen it happen before.'

Dickens smiled indulgently. 'These manifestations do not explain their mysteries in logical terms. God's power is shrouded. We have to trust.'

'I was not aware that God was pulling the strings in these particular operations.'

'As an omnipotent being He controls all things.'

'So if I plucked a book from that shelf over there and then released my grip on it and it fell to the floor, that would be one of God's mysterious scenarios?'

'A perverse example, Mr Holmes, but yes…'

'But what of Newton's well-documented theory of gravity. That is surely the rational explanation for the book falling to the ground?'

'Ah, but who gave Newton the insight, the perception, the inspiration…?'

Holmes laughed out loud. The first time I had seen him so relaxed and amused in many a long day.

Dickens responded with a grin. 'I am a zealot but I am not your typical country parson, Mr Holmes. I studied theology at Oxford and Gutenberg. I just felt I needed to seek seclusion while I worked upon, if you will forgive the immodest phrase, my magnum opus; a work that I believe will appeal and speak to all about the glory of God.'

'Even curmudgeonly sceptics like Watson and myself?'

'Especially so.'

'From our brief acquaintance, it would seem to me that if anyone could produce such a tome, I suspect that you are the man to attempt it.'

'Why, Mr Holmes, praise from you…'

Holmes waved away the unspoken compliment.

'What attracted you to Howden?' I asked in the intervening awkward silence.

Dickens shrugged. 'The post became vacant some six months ago when I was looking for… a retreat, I suppose you might call it. It is a simple country parish with its usual selection of saints and sinners. It's a fishing and farming community and the weather holds more sway than the Almighty but the villagers do pay their due respects to God. The church is always full on Sunday morning. Howden is a lovely village, gentlemen. Despite your time being limited in these parts I do recommend that you pay it a visit before leaving.'

Holmes nodded non-committally.

The clergyman rose awkwardly and snatched up his hat from the back of his chair. 'I will be on my way. I have taken too much of your time up already. I hope we meet again, gentlemen.'

'I am sure we shall,' said Holmes.

I showed the Reverend Dickens to the door and, observing that Holmes had already turned his attention to the book he had been cradling in his lap, I went outside with the cleric. 'Tell me,' I said quietly, 'has anyone gone missing from your village in the last day or two?'

Dickens looked puzzled. 'That is a strange question! Ah, don't tell me that Mr Holmes is really down here on professional business after all.'

I shook my head. 'No, no. It is just an idle enquiry, really. But do you know of such a disappearance…?'

'No, I cannot say that I do. As I intimated earlier, Howden is a quiet backwater. The first snow of winter or forked lightning in an August thunderstorm tend to be the most noticeable occurrences that ripple the still pond that is Howden.' He raised his hat. 'Good day, Doctor Watson.'

Once I had seen the cleric make his way down the garden and back onto the path that led to the track that ran along the cliffs, I hurried back indoors.

My energetic return prompted Holmes to close his book and gaze at me with interest. 'What is the matter, Watson? Something has aroused your feelings. I could tell that even as you engaged in polite conversation with our visitor.'

'I've found it. The dead body you saw yesterday. It's on the beach near a path that runs down from the cliff to the shore. It had been buried in the sand but the sea had exposed its hand and I dug... It's the same man. It fits your description exactly.'

Before I had finished talking Holmes had leapt from his chair and was pulling on his ulster.

'Good man!' he cried. 'Let's get back there straight away before it disappears again.'

It turned out that those were prophetic words. On arriving back at the beach, I found the driftwood where I had left it as a marker, but as I began to scoop the sand away, I soon realised there was nothing beneath the surface. The body had been moved again.

'It's gone!' I cried rather obviously.

'Now it's my turn to wonder whether you are losing *your* mind, Watson,' observed Holmes.

I looked at my friend horror stricken, but I observed the thin wry smile on his lips and the sardonic raise of the eyebrows. He shook his head gently. 'Fear not. I do not doubt your sanity. Nor mine if it comes to that. Whoever has committed this crime is desperate to conceal it. Without a body, our words are like the air – without substance or weight. This surprising turn of events makes me wish all the more that you had not mentioned our corpse on the beach to our visitor this morning.'

'I didn't… well, not in those terms. I merely asked… Anyway, how did you know I spoke of it?'

Holmes waved his hand at me in a dismissive fashion. 'I know you, Watson, and I know what you were trying to do. I am aware that your enquiry would be couched in your usual discreet terms. The motive was no doubt laudable but misjudged.'

'What on earth do you mean?'

'A secret shared is no longer a secret.'

'I didn't know it was a secret.'

'Well, yesterday you would have it as a self-induced hallucination.'

'Maybe… but now we do have some evidence to prove otherwise.'

'How gratifying. Cart tracks on the cliff top?'

I nodded slowly. 'And a credible theory as to why no blood was found on the path or the beach.'

'Because the corpse was carried down in a blanket which absorbed any blood from the wounds.'

'You knew already,' I snapped, beginning to feel cheated.

'I suspected that was probably the case. You may be ready to cart me off to Bedlam, Watson, but I can assure you while I admit that my emotions and my psyche are tossing on an unknown turbulent ocean at the moment, my reasoning faculties are still active and as prescient as they always were. There was a body on the beach. It was that of a murdered man. Its sudden removal was a shock to me but on reflection I now see that it was logical.'

'Logical?'

'It was a murder that was never meant to be discovered.'

'All murders are discovered in the end.'

'You sound like an evangelistic preacher, Watson. In every case, the perpetrator of a murder wishes to remain anonymous – that applies to the ruffian who clubs to death a toff in the east end of London for his watch or the bored aristocrat who poisons his wife in order to free himself from the shackles of a loveless marriage. But there are some murders which are never meant to be recognised as such. I believe our man on the beach is of this category.'

I groaned out loud and my patience snapped. 'Why, oh why, is it that whenever you have a theory you present it to me in the most obscure way. All you give me are Sherlock Holmes hieroglyphics for my meagre brain to tackle. I really don't know what you are talking about and what infuriates me is that you know I don't know.'

Holmes leaned forward and thrust his face into mine. 'So, I am behaving normally then?'

My mouth opened to speak but then I caught that mischievous glint in his eye. My angry utterance turned into a chuckle and Holmes joined me. Before long we were both laughing heartily.

'If you were so certain that a murder had been committed, why on earth didn't you take action? Surely the police should be informed.' I shouted my words at Holmes above the whistle of the salty wind which had risen suddenly and blew into our faces.

'As I read the matter, Watson, there are two possible theories as to why the body was being disposed of in such a way.'

'Thrown into the sea, you mean.'

'Yes. Either the murderers were getting rid of the corpse so that its discovery would not implicate them in the crime because a missing person is not a murdered person. Anyone can go missing. In a fishing and farming community there will be many transient workers who are here one day and gone the next. There is nothing really suspicious in that. However, murder attracts attention. Little happens around here and unlike London, where casual homicides are all too common, a murder would be a major upheaval, inviting the police, the authorities, the press – unwelcome strangers.'

'So the killers are locals.'

'So I read the riddle. Local men who have no intention of moving away. But now they have a problem.'

'Which is?'

'We have seen their handiwork. No matter how skilfully they covered their tracks, they know we saw the body. That is their problem.'

'What do you think they'll do about it?'

'Bide their time. Watch and wait to see what we do.'

'Watch? You think we are being watched?' I gazed around the windswept terrain, barren and deserted as far as the eye could see.

'Monitored at least.'

Suddenly a thought struck me. 'And that is why you didn't want me to mention your discovery to anyone…'

'However obliquely. It was our secret but now it isn't.'

'But I only asked if the Reverend knew of any missing persons hereabouts.'

'And no doubt piqued his curiosity.'

'Well… yes.'

'And this confirmed that we were in possession of deadly knowledge. We know that a man has gone missing and that a man has been brutally murdered.'

'But my question was to a man of the church.'

Holmes took my arm and gently swung me around so that we could retrace our steps back to the cottage.

'Tell me, Watson, did you notice the fire when you returned to the cottage?'

'The fire...' I said with some surprise at this change of direction in our conversation.

'The one in the fireplace,' he added dryly.

'Yes, I think so.'

'How was it?'

'Somewhat feeble. I assumed it had only just been lit. Very little flame.'

'Bravo. You saw and observed. Very little flame... or smoke for that matter.'

'Hardly any,' I replied, wondering if Holmes' mind was slipping once again.

'I would agree with you. There were just a few insubstantial vapours. Certainly there was not enough smoke to billow from our chimney pot to announce to the world that the cottage was occupied. Was there?'

Five

$\mathcal{O}$

From Dr Watson's Journal

On arriving back at the cottage, Holmes consulted his pocket watch. 'Nearly lunchtime. Our little excursion has sharpened my appetite. And you certainly must be hungry, old fellow, not having had any breakfast today. What do you say we take lunch in a hostelry in Howden? However small the village, if there's a church there is bound to be an inn – refuges for both saints and sinners. Let us see if the place lives up to the Reverend Dickens' recommendations.'

I rubbed my chin. 'Give me time to have a proper shave,' said I, making for the stairs. 'I'll be with you shortly.'

'I'll harness up the nag and prepare the cart in readiness,' replied Holmes.

By the time I had scraped a razor across my face and slipped on a fresh collar, Holmes had brought the cart round to the front of the cottage, ready for our journey. It was as I was locking up that I saw them. White marks near the bottom of the door. A row of five images chalked in a crude and childish manner. I was immediately reminded of the stick figures that we had encountered in the case I called 'The

Dancing Men' – matchstick men each representing a letter of the alphabet which spelt out a warning message. But on closer inspection I saw that these markings were a series of queer and somehow unsettling symbols that seemed to have no similarity to each other. Something made me shiver inside as I observed them.

Suddenly a shadow fell over me. It was Sherlock Holmes. 'What is it, Watson?'

Mutely, I pointed to the images. He knelt beside me and scrutinised the chalk marks. 'Well, they're fresh and they certainly weren't here yesterday.'

'What are they and what do they mean?'

'They appear to be some kind of runic symbol but I have no idea what they signify. However, I suspect they do not spell out a message of welcome.'

'Who put them there?'

Holmes raised a sardonic eyebrow. 'We have not had many visitors.'

'You cannot be suggesting that the Reverend Dickens chalked these marks here.'

'There is too little data to ascertain that,' he replied, taking a pencil and notepad from his pocket. Carefully he made a copy of the five symbols. 'But,' he continued, once his task was complete, 'at present our clerical friend would seem to be the most likely candidate.'

Less than half an hour later we were in Howden. Our journey for the most part had been travelled in silence. We were both deep in thought about the vague mystery which now seemed to be impinging on our lives. A man had been murdered and his body disposed of in such a way, if Holmes was right, that would make it look as though the man had just left the area. Disappeared, without leaving a trace. We had no notion of who he was, where he came from and why he was killed –

or, for that matter, who the murderers might be. Everything about the situation was intangible. It also appeared that the cottage was being watched. It seemed to me that in some strange way our knowledge of the crime had probably placed our lives at risk. And then there were the strange symbols on the cottage door. I could not remember a situation which was so baffling; there really were no obvious roads of enquiry open to us. It seemed to me that we were in the unhappy situation of having to wait to see what would happen next.

Holmes' features betrayed none of his thoughts but I, who knew him of old, was certain he was turning over each item of evidence, each vague piece in this puzzle, in his mind, searching for a way forward. I was uncertain how he viewed this challenge. Was he frightened that, in his current state of mental health, he might not be capable of tackling the mystery? Or, indeed, was it just the sort of conundrum that would revive his faculties?

The village of Howden was indeed small, consisting of one broad unmade thoroughfare, with quaint honey-coloured medieval buildings running in a higgledy-piggledy fashion down either side of it. When we arrived, the village was as still as a painting. It was nearly one o'clock and the sun had broken through the thin cloud and bathed everything in a pale yellow sheen, which increased the impression that one had stepped back in time to an earlier age. I fully expected to see some ancient rustic emerge from one of the time-worn doors and step into the street. Apart from a stray cat and a cluster of chickens in someone's garden the place seemed deserted.

'The *Marie Celeste* of villages, Watson,' said Holmes, breaking his silence at last.

'Yes. Quiet as the grave.'

Just as I made this observation I heard a great raucous cry of voices at the far end of the street, and then beyond the great bole of an ancient oak tree a group of men appeared apparently from nowhere, the dust of the street clouding up around them. The men formed a circle around two of their brothers, who looked as though they were in the process of a fight.

'I think we have found our inn, Watson,' grinned Holmes, gently encouraging our steed to increase his pace. As we neared the group, I observed the inn sign which had been hidden by the leafy branches of the oak tree. The faded lettering proclaimed it to be The Dark Man.

We dismounted and Holmes tied the horse to a ring fixed in the wall beside the inn. As our presence was observed, the fight stopped and all the men turned their heads in our direction. There were nine in all, including the opponents, all dressed in rough cord trousers and thick twill shirts. Farm labourers getting overheated after a lunchtime drink, no doubt.

'Good day, gentlemen,' said Holmes.

Nine pairs of cold, suspicious eyes stared back at us with no word spoken. And then the younger and burlier of the fighters, taking the opportunity to catch his opponent off guard, swung his giant fist and knocked him to the ground. He landed in a shower of dust and cursed loudly as blood spurted from his nose. This seemed to break the spell and the fight resumed, with the rest turning their back on us to shout encouragement to their favourite combatant.

I surveyed the spectators and for some reason my eye was drawn to the shoes of one of them, a large man with a moustache and mean-spirited eyes. The buckle of his right shoe was missing. Instinctively my hand reached into my coat pocket and grasped the buckle I had found on the path leading to the beach. I inspected it quickly and surreptitiously, long enough to ascertain that it appeared to be the same size and design. Holmes had observed my actions and he gave me a knowing nod of the head. I slipped the buckle back in my pocket.

We entered the cool interior of the inn. It was a rough and basic sort of establishment, dimly lighted with coarse wooden tables and benches and an uneven flagged floor. The landlord, a large fellow with a shock of flaxen hair, was leaning on the far end of the bar in conversation with a red-faced man wearing a long stained smock. Neither man acknowledged our entrance. Holmes approached the bar and smiled at the landlord, who ignored the gesture and carried on talking. My friend slipped a coin from his pocket and, placing it on the counter, he spun it around. It whirled noisily on the wooden surface. Just before the coin lost its momentum, Holmes slapped his hand down hard on top of it. The noise echoed loudly in the dingy room. The landlord, surprised by the sound, turned his head.

'Ah,' cried Holmes, fixing him with his penetrating gaze, 'my friend and I would like to buy a glass of beer and some food, if you would be so kind.'

With a stiff and surly reluctance, the landlord left his associate. 'I can do you the ale, mister, but we ain't got no food.'

'We ask for nothing fancy, you understand. Bread and cheese would suffice.'

The landlord shook his head. 'No food.'

'Now that is surprising, Mr Henshaw…'

He narrowed his eyes. 'You know my name.' The man seemed concerned that his identity had been discovered.

'It is above the door outside.'

The man paused. 'What do you want here?'

'As I explained, some ale and some bread and cheese. I was assured by our friend the Reverend Dickens…'

At the mention of this name, Henshaw's eyes flashed with a sudden interest. 'What about him?'

'He assured us that we should find a welcome here. Good food and good ale is what he said.'

The fellow in the smock spat noisily on the stone floor.

The landlord leaned over the bar nearer Holmes, his roughly hewn face thrust forward. 'I don't know who you are, mister, and I don't care. My licence obliges me to serve you ale if you requests it, but as I said we ain't got no food. And if you'd take my advice – and I really think you ought – you and your friend had best be on your way. We don't take to strangers here.'

'Henshaw, shut your mouth and serve these gentlemen with a glass of Roses ale… on the house.'

The voice, sharp and authoritative, came from the shadows in the darkest part of the bar parlour behind us. Its effect was instantaneous. The recalcitrant landlord froze for a moment and then retrieved two fresh glasses from below the bar and in a desultory fashion began filling them from one of the large barrels behind the bar counter. We turned to face the owner of the voice as he rose from his seat, emerging from the shadows, and approached us. He was a young man, not yet thirty, dressed in the clothes of a country squire. His thick black hair was swept back in a puritan fashion, exposing a cruelly handsome visage with a smooth aquiline nose and a fleshy sensual mouth which curled into a smile as he extended his hand to Holmes.

'I apologise for this rather rude welcome. Mr Henshaw is unaccustomed to strangers and tends to react in an aggressive fashion. Please forgive him. He is a good-hearted soul, if a little restricted in the practice of polite manners and social graces.' He turned to face the landlord, who had now placed two glasses of ale on the bar for us. 'Isn't that so, Jacob?'

Henshaw said nothing but gave a reluctant nod.

'Come, gentlemen, join me at my table and then once your thirst has been quenched, I shall make amends for the limitations of The Dark Man. You must come to my house for some sustenance. We cannot have you leave Howden with tales of inhospitality.'

'You are most kind,' said Holmes, bowing his head, 'Mr...'

'Blackwood, sir, Enoch Blackwood at your service.' He sat at his table and bade us do likewise. We introduced ourselves but I derived the distinct impression that Blackwood already knew who we were.

'I presume,' said he, 'that you are *the* Sherlock Holmes and Doctor Watson, the criminologists.'

Holmes chuckled. 'I have never heard ourselves referred to in such terms.'

'I have read your accounts with great interest, Doctor Watson. Although I am domiciled in this quiet part of the country, I pride myself on keeping up to date with all the latest gossip and events in London. I travel up to town for a few days once every month or so to make sure my brain does not rot down here. I do get bored and starved of stimulation – intelligent conversation – so you gentlemen would be doing me a great favour by taking lunch with me.'

'You have business in the area?'

'You could say that,' he grinned. 'I own much of the land to the north of the village – there are two farms and several houses as well as this establishment, the revenue from which keeps me in the manner to which I am almost accustomed.' He laughed again and then drained his glass. 'My father, who is no longer with us in the flesh, was Bartholomew Blackwood. You have no doubt heard of him, Mr Holmes.'

Holmes froze, his glass tilted towards his mouth. 'Indeed, I have.'

'Then perhaps that answers your unasked question. Why someone like myself allows himself to vegetate in a little village in the middle of nowhere. As the offspring of the Devil's Companion, I have little choice.'

Six

From Dr Watson's Journal

I, too, had heard of Bartholomew Blackwood. There were few educated men who did not know the name and the notorious story of the self-proclaimed Devil worshipper. He had died somewhere in England several years ago – or so it was believed. It was never known where the foul creature had found his final resting ground, but it would now seem that somehow Bartholomew Blackwood had made his last refuge in Howden and that his son, Enoch, had inherited his land and property. Apart from the wealth that Bartholomew Blackwood had accumulated over the years from rich patrons of his satanic cult, The Fellowship of the Dark Dawn, the son had been left a terrible legacy. He was the offspring of one of the most evil and despised men that had ever lived.

'I trust that I have not shocked you with my revelation. In the past I have had men spit at me because of my heritage. It is a burden I have grown used to.' He shrugged his shoulders and gave us a gentle smile but it was one without humour or warmth. 'All I can do is assure you that I do not follow the beliefs of... the man whose name I bear.'

'I'm afraid that society is always keen to assume the worst of men,' observed Holmes tartly.

Blackwood nodded. 'Bearing that truth in mind, I trust you will still join me for lunch.'

'That is very kind, eh, Watson?'

'Indeed,' I responded with as much veracity as I could muster.

'Excellent!' Blackwood cried, rising swiftly.

We followed Enoch Blackwood out of The Dark Man into the sunshine. The fighting ruffians, no doubt tired of their boorish antics, had all dispersed apart from two of their company who sat against the inn wall, knees hunched up against their chests, engaged in casual conversation. I noticed that one of them was the fellow with the missing buckle.

'Is that your cart?' asked Blackwood.

Holmes nodded. 'We have travelled here from Samphire Cottage.'

'Ah, so you're staying there are you?'

'Until the end of the week,' I responded.

'I'll get these chaps to bring the cart up to the house. We can walk in the sunshine. It will not take us more than ten minutes.' So saying, Blackwood strolled over to the men lazing by the inn and, bending down, engaged them in a brief, hushed conversation. There were nods of agreement as he tossed them a coin.

'That's settled,' he said beaming, rejoining us. 'This way, gentlemen.'

He led us to the farther end of the village, where the road narrowed. We turned into a side lane where the rich foliage encroached on the simple man-made route.

'I take it that you do not live alone, Mr Blackwood,' said Holmes, snapping off the slender branch from an overhanging chestnut and swinging it like a cane.

'Now why do you say that?'

'A man of note in the community must have servants.'

'Even coin cannot persuade the fearful. I have no servants. My reputation – or at least the name of Blackwood – determines that. But I have my sister who is devoted to me, as I am to her. Arabella. She sees to our domestic arrangements. We muddle along together. You will forgive me for being honest but my much-misguided father left us with a cursed legacy that has blighted our lives. We are unclean. Pariahs in our own country. In this backwater at least we are tolerated because of our wealth, but we are also feared and hated. Perhaps you are now having some misgivings about visiting our home.'

Holmes slashed the air with the branch. 'Such thoughts had not entered my mind. I am not an advocate of the theory that the sins of the father are inherited…'

Blackwood gave a hoarse laugh. 'I knew that you were a man of enlightenment. And what of you, Doctor Watson? What are your feelings on the matter?' he asked with some seriousness.

'I have always judged a man on his own merits, Mr Blackwood.' I realised that my rather frosty demeanour in delivering this observation robbed it of some of its genuine sentiment. In one sense I felt sorry for any man damned by the behaviour and reputation of others in his family, but I had to admit to myself that there was something about Enoch Blackwood that I did not like and which made me feel uncomfortable.

Blackwood did not notice, or at least pretended not to notice my reserve. 'I am pleased to hear it,' he said heartily. 'It is good to encounter two men who do not believe that I will transform them into goblins' or witches' familiars on a whim.'

'Have you never thought of selling up and moving to another part of the country where your name is not known?' I asked.

Blackwood skipped round and began walking backwards as he addressed me. 'Is there anywhere that does not know the cursed name of Blackwood?'

'Then change it?' said Holmes.

'Ah, if it were so simple. I change it and I lose everything – we lose everything, Arabella and I.'

'Your father's will?'

'Indeed. He was determined that the family name should live on. The tyranny doesn't end there. Either Arabella or I have to produce a male child by the time we are thirty or… poof!' He threw his arms dramatically into the air like a stage magician concluding his act. 'Our land, our inheritance, the clothes from our backs are forfeit. We are prisoners of our own inheritance.'

'There is no legal means to break this will?'

Blackwood's features darkened. 'Do you not think we have tried? I have scoured the Temple for a legal brain with the cunning and expertise to smash the thing to smithereens – to no avail. And time is running out. The clock is ticking ever louder and the hands are spinning around the face of the clock.'

The lane grew darker as the trees thickened; their overhanging branches rich with summer greenery created a barrier against the sky with only fierce yellow beams of sunlight tigering the way before us. In the burgeoning heat and amid the buzzing throb of insects I had the sensation that I was leaving the real world behind. The warm air pressed in on me and the shifting foliage softened into a sheet of variegated green, rippling before my eyes. My vision blurred and I began to feel light-headed, dizzy, uncertain of my footsteps. The rustle of the leaves resonated loudly in my ear. I put my condition down to the potent ale I had just supped in The Dark Man. It certainly had a most strange but not unpleasing honeyed taste. Holmes had drunk little, but I had drained my glass.

Trickles of sweat ran down my brow and the world shimmered before me through a veil-like haze. In the background I could hear the drone of conversation between Holmes and Blackwood, the steady regular tones of my friend contrasting with the dramatic rise and fall of our new companion's, but the voices seemed distant and not part of my experience. It was as though I were slipping into a dream. My eyelids began to feel heavy and drooped, dimming my vision even more.

'You all right, old boy?' I heard my friend's voice break through the drowsy hum. Holmes came near me and touched my elbow. I shook my head and blinked. My vision sharpened and my drowsiness gradually evaporated.

'Here we are!' cried Blackwood. 'Home sweet home.' He darted ahead of us and, beckoning us forward, he turned into an almost hidden driveway. We followed him down a tunnel of overgrown trees to a house gothic in style but modest in proportions. The rampant ivy which clung to its walls had almost claimed it for its own.

'One might easily miss such a dwelling,' observed my friend.

'Many do, Mr Holmes. And it is probably as well.'

Sprinting forward, Blackwood cupped his hands to his mouth and produced an eerie whistling sound. It filled the air, echoing in the surrounding trees. As the sound died away, Blackwood made the noise again. For a second time the strange high-pitched notes reverberated on the warm air, sending a brace of wood pigeons spiralling skywards from a nearby oak tree.

The door of the house opened and a figure emerged.

A young woman with long, dark lustrous hair, wearing a simple cream linen dress, stepped from the darkness of the house. Her pale, haunted features quivered with uncertainty until she saw Blackwood and then, remarkably, she cupped her slender fingers to her lips and produced the same strange whistle.

Blackwood laughed and then the girl ran to him and embraced him.

'My sister, Arabella,' he said, turning to us while his arms enfolded her.

The girl smiled at us. She did look remarkably like her brother in many ways – the dark hair, the long slender nose and the arched eyebrows – but she did not radiate his ebullience.

'We have distinguished visitors for lunch, my dear. This is Mr Sherlock Holmes, the famous detective and his companion, the writer Doctor Watson.'

Arabella Blackwood did not quite know how to react to this news. It was clear to me that she was unaccustomed to any visitors arriving on her doorstep, let alone a pair of strangers who were presented to her as being 'distinguished'.

'You are welcome,' she said demurely, and then, turning to her brother, she addressed him more sharply. 'Enoch, you might have let me know we were to have company. I have nothing prepared.'

'I didn't know myself until about fifteen minutes ago. I rescued these gentlemen from the rudeness of Henshaw.'

At this point Holmes stepped forward and gave a curt bow. 'Some bread and cheese would suffice, Miss Blackwood.'

Holmes' intervention seemed to bring a change in the girl's demeanour. She smiled again, but this time there was genuine warmth in the gesture. 'I think we can manage something a little more interesting than bread and cheese. How about omelettes with some home-grown vegetables?'

'Excellent,' said Holmes.

Enoch Blackwood gave a cry of pleasure and hugged his sister again. 'Ah, Bella, I knew you'd be fine with it.'

She kissed her brother and grinned broadly. 'Now you take our visitors on to the lawn for a seat in the sunshine while I organise things in the kitchen.'

'Of course,' he cried, and beckoned us to follow him around to the front of the house as Arabella ran back indoors.

Turning the corner of the building we came upon a large unkempt lawn that ran away in a gentle slope to a copse which seemed to surround the property on three sides. A wicker table and several decrepit chairs were situated on the lawn. Enoch Blackwood bade us take a seat. Holmes lit his pipe and puffed on it contentedly. We sat for some time without speaking, entranced in some way by the quiet beauty of the surroundings. The faint hum of errant bees, the odd cry of some invisible bird and the gentle rustling of the trees were the only sounds one could hear.

'When did your father die?' asked Holmes at length, stretching out his long legs.

'Some eight years ago. On the eve of my twentieth birthday.'

'And where is he buried? In the churchyard here?'

Blackwood gave a sardonic chuckle. 'You will forgive me, Mr Holmes, but that is a family secret. I am aware that you are a man of honour, but shared secrets have a way of becoming known. There are those who would give much to know the whereabouts of my father, to perform horrendous rites on his remains. Whatever he did in life, I wish him to rest in peace.'

Holmes nodded judiciously. 'I apologise for asking. I realise that what for me was an idle enquiry for you is a very serious matter indeed.'

Suddenly the air was filled with the strange whistling sound again.

'Ah, that means our lunch is ready. Come along, gentlemen.'

Blackwood led us back to the house, where we were shown into a small, dark, cluttered room housing a large dining table and six chairs which seemed to dwarf the proportions of the chamber. Outside, foliage pressed against the grimy windows as though desperate to gain entry. As a result the room received little natural light, and it was necessary for two large candelabra to be lighted in order to provide sufficient illumination to allow us to dine. There were several works of art adorning the walls – oil paintings mostly of strange and mysterious landscapes. One striking piece over the fireplace showed some underground chamber into which a shaft of pale light fell, spotlighting a sinewy arm stretching out from the earth, its fingers running with dark red blood. Blackwood saw me glance uncomfortably at this strange and unnerving picture.

'My father painted that,' he said. 'As he did most of the artwork in this house. As you can see he had talent but, as you might expect, his subjects were dark and… unusual.'

'You should show them some of your paintings later, Enoch,' said Arabella.

'I'm sure these good gentlemen would not be interested in the works of a careless amateur.'

'On the contrary,' I said with forced politeness. 'We should be greatly interested, eh, Holmes?'

My friend turned to me so that his face was hidden from our hosts and raised an ironic eyebrow. He knew very well that my interest in art was virtually non-existent.

'That would be most interesting,' he said evenly with a fixed smile.

The meal was simple but delicious. Holmes, Blackwood and Arabella took a glass of hock with their food, but after my experience in the lane, I declined the wine and just had a glass of water. The conversation was stilted, with some awkward silences. Holmes casually kept returning to the subject of Blackwood's father but like an expert batsman, Enoch Blackwood deflected these enquiries with a deft accuracy. He was obviously well practised in dealing with those who tried to find out more than he was prepared to divulge.

While this was going on, I observed Arabella. She ate little and spent most of the meal staring at her brother with a kind of childlike adoration. She was indeed an attractive young lady but there was something about her manner that seemed odd, as though she were in some kind of trance. It was the sort of behaviour I had observed in

Holmes when he was coming out of one of his cocaine stupors. On one occasion she caught me looking at her and she smiled at me in a fey fashion, but somehow it seemed a calculated action, as though she were trying to persuade me of her vulnerability, a vulnerability that was not real.

By the time the meal was over, I was eager to leave these two rather strange individuals to their dark untidy quarters and their sad but chilling legacy.

In an obvious fashion I consulted my pocket watch. 'I think, Holmes,' said I, 'that it is time we left these good people to their own affairs. We have imposed upon their hospitality for far too long.'

Holmes nodded in agreement and we both rose to go, but Arabella took this as a signal to jump to her feet. 'You cannot leave!' she cried, addressing us with the petulant ferocity of an infant, her eyes wild with emotion. 'You cannot leave,' she repeated, more softly. 'Not until you have seen Enoch's paintings.'

'By all means,' smiled Holmes urbanely with a casual politeness that defused the tension of the moment.

'I am sorry, gentlemen,' said Enoch Blackwood. 'My sister is so passionate about my artistic endeavours. She sees far more value in my canvases than I do, or I suspect an art dealer would do.'

'Please take a look at them,' cried Arabella. It was the bleat of a young child.

Enoch led us into the hall and up two flights of stairs to the top storey of the house. Arabella followed in our wake. On the little landing there, Holmes turned to face the room on the left of us.

'No!' exclaimed Blackwood sharply. 'Not there. Not that room. It is here. My studio is here.' He strode quickly to the room located on the right and unlocked it. We were led into a spacious attic area with a large window set into the sloping roof which flooded the room with light. There was an easel placed directly under the window on which was a large unfinished watercolour. It represented a church at dusk. The stained-glass windows glowed in the gloom, illuminated from within, and a flock of birds were pictured about to roost in the large oak tree by the lychgate. In the porch of the church, by the open door, a tall figure in what looked like a monk's habit was silhouetted, his back to the viewer.

'That is my latest effort. It is unfinished but I am not particularly happy with the tree. It is, I believe, a little too big and the foliage is not quite natural enough. As you can see with this and my other efforts' – he indicated a range of paintings propped up against the wall around the studio – 'they are modest pieces at best, but the very activity of painting is soothing to me. I become lost in the scene I am creating and it provides me some peace and solace.'

Holmes picked up one of the paintings and examined it. It was another landscape. This time it was one of cliffs and sea. I looked over my friend's shoulder to share his view. With my limited knowledge of art, it seemed to me that Blackwood had captured the fury of the waves as they crashed against the rocks at the base of the cliffs with great effectiveness. As my eye scanned the picture, I noticed that at the top left-hand corner, where the cliff top was at its most rugged, there was the same silhouetted figure that had featured in the other painting. This time, the figure appeared to be staring out to sea, the grey, fiercely turbulent sea.

'These may not have the genius of Constable but they are very fine, Mr Blackwood,' said Holmes, replacing the painting. 'I have seen similar works of art in the galleries of Bond Street at very respectable sums.'

'You see, Enoch. I told you they were good,' cried Arabella, stepping forward. 'You should try to sell some.'

Blackwood smiled gently and ruffled his sister's hair. 'Maybe,' he said and then turned to Holmes. 'I thank you for your honest opinion, sir.'

'It is the opinion of an enthusiast, merely an amateur critic. But now I do believe it is time we were away.'

We said our farewell to Arabella at the front door and Blackwood escorted us to the gate, where our horse and cart were waiting for us. We thanked Blackwood again for his help and hospitality and then, with Holmes in charge of the reins, we headed back towards the village.

Seven

From Dr Watson's Journal

As we rattled down the lane to the village in the cart, the horse plodding along in a lethargic fashion, the leaves of the overhanging trees occasionally brushing our faces, Holmes was strangely silent. I had fully expected him to analyse our encounter with Enoch Blackwood and his sister and elicit my reactions to this odd couple but instead he seemed to be lost in his own thoughts. As we rounded the sharp curve that joined the main street of Howden, I decided to take the lead and initiate a response from my friend.

'I should say there is some mental instability with the girl, Arabella,' I observed casually.

'Indeed,' said Holmes after a pause, rousing himself from his reverie. 'In both sister *and* brother I should say, and it is hardly surprising given their parentage and situation. It is a cursed inheritance. But, more particularly, there were some unusual aspects of our meeting which intrigue me.'

'Do share them with me.'

'In due course, but first I wish to take a look at the church.' So saying, Holmes pulled the cart to the side of the road and began to dismount.

I followed suit and after hitching the horse we strolled together towards the lychgate that led to the grounds of the church.

'Do you recognise it?' Holmes asked, as we passed through the gate.

'Yes, it is the church in Blackwood's painting.'

It was a rough-stoned Norman edifice which had seen better days. The stonework was crumbling and the rampant ivy was beginning to cover the stained-glass windows. The whole building had an air of dereliction about it.

'The state of the place hardly reflects the Reverend Dickens' claim that the church is full every Sunday. No one seems to care about the place at all.'

'Quite so,' said Holmes in a distracted fashion, his mind obviously elsewhere as he gazed intently at the stained-glass window close to the entrance.

The graveyard was also greatly overgrown; tall grasses had conquered, almost obliterating many of the gravestones. Stepping off the path into this small wild jungle of weeds, Holmes examined some of them. 'No recent burials, it would seem,' he observed. 'The folk around here must have the secret of longevity.'

He returned to the pathway and we progressed to the church door.

It was locked.

'I thought God's house was always open,' I said.

'Perhaps there are some secrets within.'

'What do you mean by that?'

Holmes chuckled. 'I'm not sure. But there is a deep dark mystery surrounding us here, Watson. We have been drawn into something quite recherché. Something very puzzling. Gone is your relaxing, recuperative holiday, I am afraid.'

He stopped suddenly and gazed up at the row of trees which bordered the perimeter of the churchyard. 'Listen,' he said in an urgent whisper.

I did as he asked but I could not hear anything. I conveyed this confession to him. He smiled bleakly. 'Precisely,' he said. 'There are no birds singing here.'

Without further words, we wandered back down the path together to the waiting cart. We were just about to board when my attention was caught by some movement to my right, far down the deserted street. Like an image in a shimmering mirage I observed a figure rushing towards us. At first it was just a dark blur, held slightly out of focus, but as it grew nearer I saw to my astonishment that it was Arabella Blackwood. She was running as though her life depended upon it. Her dark hair streamed behind her and her thin face was set in an expression of grim determination. As she grew close she waved to us, and emitted a shrill cry: 'Wait!'

Holmes took a few paces forward to meet her. She arrived at his side, her face misted in perspiration and her eyes flashing with strong emotion. It took her a moment to catch her breath and then she clasped Holmes by the hand. 'Get away from here,' she said, her voice low and passionate. 'Do you hear me? Get away. They mean to kill you.'

Before Holmes could respond, she had turned on her heel and was racing back down the street in the direction from which she had come.

My friend, who seemed completely unfazed by this strange warning, gave one of his cold enigmatic smiles. 'Curiouser and curiouser, eh, Watson?'

'Shall we go after her?'

Holmes shook his head. 'There will be little point in doing that at the moment. She will not tell us more. And anyway, perhaps that is what she expects us to do.'

'What on earth do you mean by that?' I asked in surprise.

My friend chuckled. 'An instinct, I'm afraid. But one born of experience in dealing with dark matters. There are too many riddles for us to solve at the moment. I have the impression that we are being played with and I certainly am not happy in the role of puppet. Arabella's warning is certainly one that we shall ignore. All we can do for the present is to store that little moment along with all the other strange incidents that we have experienced in the last twenty-four hours in the hope that we may in due course of time be able to make some sense of them.'

He looked down the empty street, darkening now with late afternoon shadows. 'There is no one about,' he observed quietly, 'and yet why do I have the impression that we are being watched?'

We returned to the cottage in silence, each lost in our own thoughts. It seemed to me that since Holmes had discovered the body on the beach our lives had entered a kind of dreamlike dimension. The appearing and disappearing corpse, the weird images chalked on our door, the inhospitable nature of the villagers, the strange brother and sister and her implicit warning – they were all puzzling surreal fragments in an enigmatic tapestry, the complete design of which was hidden from us.

It was twilight when we reached our little holiday home. Together we stabled and fed the horse before going inside the cottage, where there was another shock awaiting us. I had just lit the lamp when I saw it: a shadowy figure slumped in the chair by the fireplace. I gave a cry of surprise and Holmes, who was hanging up his hat and coat in the hall, rushed to my side. In the pale yellow light cast by the lamp we observed the body of a corpse – *the* corpse, the man whom I had discovered buried on the beach. His head lay slumped slightly against the wing of the chair but his dead eyes were open, staring sightlessly at the ceiling. Spots of crusted blood stained the front of his white shirt.

Holmes moved forward and knelt down by the figure, examining his hands and the wound at the back of his head.

At length, he turned to me, his features taut and exultant, his eyes glittering darkly. 'They are playing with us now, Watson.'

'Who are? And what do "they" hope to achieve?'

'I am afraid at the moment I cannot answer either question. However, if you would be so good as to go to the bookcase by the window and extract a small blue volume from the top shelf – the one entitled *Flowers and Fauna of the Devon Coast* – I think I may be able to shed a little light on the identity of our unexpected guest.'

I knew in situations like this it was pointless querying such a strange request, and so I did as I was asked and passed Holmes the required volume.

'I was perusing this earlier today,' he said as he opened the book on the title page and passed it to me. Beneath the title was the author's name, 'The Rev Simon Dickens, Vicar of the Parish of Howden'. Below this was a vignette of the author himself.

'Recognise the fellow?' asked Holmes smoothly.

The hairs on the back of my neck tingled. There was no doubt about it. The sketch was the exact likeness of the dead man lolling in the armchair by our hearth. My astonished gaze answered my friend's question.

'Without doubt, he is the Reverend Simon Dickens… late of this parish,' said Holmes.

'And he has been murdered.'

'He has.'

'Then who was that fellow who visited us this morning…?'

'Another query to which I cannot provide a full answer. Obviously it was not *the* Reverend Simon Dickens. It would seem that he is a kind of replacement, an imposter. Some of what he told us may be true, but certainly the fellow we encountered this morning is not the genuine article.'

'You mean he murdered the real Dickens in order to take his place.'

Holmes shrugged. 'It's not clear whether he actually carried out the fatal blow or was even there when this poor fellow was struck down, but the most interesting aspect of this business is the implied complicity.'

'I do not understand.'

'You cannot remove a cleric and bring in a substitute without the knowledge and agreed involvement of many others. Such a recognisable character around the village. He disappears one day and the next his replacement takes over. Questions, serious questions are bound to be asked... unless...'

'Unless what?'

'Unless...' Holmes paused and I observed a strange emotion register in his eyes. 'It is almost too fantastic to contemplate.' He shook his head as though he was trying to dislodge this dark notion.

'Share your thoughts with me at least.'

'What if the whole village knew of the murder? Not only knew of it but... actually condoned it.'

'That is too fantastic... surely?'

Holmes nodded. 'Strange indeed. Unique in my experience, but while highly improbable it is not impossible. At the moment, it seems to be the only solution that fits the conundrum. As I intimated, we are woefully short of data.'

I glanced once more at the body in the chair. 'We shall have to inform the police now. At least we have proof that a murder has been committed.'

'Indeed. We shall have to travel to Totnes with the body in the morning and contact the constabulary there. There is no regular policeman in the village. That's of course as long as this fellow does not get up in the night and disappear again.'

I shuddered at the thought. 'Let's move him to the spare bedroom and lock him there for safety's sake until the morning.'

Holmes complied with my suggestion and we bore the body away and laid him down on the bed in the smallest bedroom. Holmes covered him with a sheet and we drew the curtains, before locking the door.

Some thirty minutes later, we sat around the hearth as the newly laid fire struggled to turn itself into a blaze. We both cradled glasses of brandy in our hands and stared at the feeble yellow tongues of flame as they licked at the recalcitrant logs.

'Why would they want to kill the vicar and put another man in his place?' I asked.

'There are several possibilities. Obviously the Reverend Dickens would not fall in with their plans and so had to be eliminated. Perhaps they just wanted a puppet in charge of the church. Or perhaps they needed a clergyman of a different persuasion.'

'What on earth do you mean by that?' I asked, unnerved because I suspected that I knew the answer.

'I am thinking of Bartholomew Blackwood and his legacy.'

'So you think that Enoch and Arabella Blackwood are involved in this strange business.'

'Involved, yes. In some way, willingly or otherwise. Unfortunately I cannot build my house with straw. There is still much to learn and much to discover before we can construct a reasonable theory as to what is behind this puzzling affair. For now we must await further developments while keeping our senses on full alert.'

I slept fitfully that night, and when I did I was haunted by strange dreams including walking corpses and the figure of Bartholomew Blackwood emerging from an overgrown grave in the churchyard, his white bony fingers reaching for my neck. I was glad when I saw pale light begin to struggle into the room through the drawn curtains, indicating that dawn was here at last. I carried out my ablutions quickly and on entering the sitting room, I found Holmes sitting by the hearth where I had left him the night before. He was staring at the dead grey ashes in the grate as he puffed with some dedication upon his pipe.

'Have you been here all night?' I asked.

My friend gave a start and pulled himself out of his reverie. 'Ah, Watson, is it morning already?'

'It is,' I said, drawing back the curtains, allowing light to flood the room.

'I have been thinking. Trying to make some sense of it all.'

'And have you?'

He gave me a bleak smile. 'I don't know… yet.'

'I'll make us some hot tea.'

'That would be wonderful,' Holmes said, rising to his feet and stretching. 'If you could conjure up a couple of boiled eggs also… In the meantime I'll wash and shave and spruce myself up for the day ahead. It promises to be an interesting one.'

Half an hour later we were sitting around the rough wooden table in the tiny kitchen of the cottage devouring boiled eggs and tea and toast. Holmes looked pale and drawn; dark circles beneath his eyes gave evidence of his sleepless night, but his manner was bright and ebullient.

'Do you believe in coincidences?' he asked at length, pushing away his empty plate and lighting a cigarette.

'Within reason, yes. Fate can play many strange tricks, I suppose. What coincidence had you in mind?'

'That game of billiards at your club with the fellow Cawthorne. The new member who quickly latched on to you and very soon brought up my name.'

'What about him?'

'It was on his recommendation that we ended up here. As I understand it, he arranged all the finances for us. You had no direct dealing with the owner. In fact we don't know who the actual owner of this property is, do we?'

I shook my head slowly.

'Objectively, the whole arrangement was rather strange and hurried. A man you do not know very well recommends a cottage for the recuperation of an ailing friend and secures and organises the tenure for you.'

'He was just being considerate. His wife benefited from a quiet stay here.'

'So he told you. There's no evidence of that, is there? There's no evidence, in fact, that the man was married.'

'I took him at his word. The word of a gentleman.'

Holmes smiled sardonically. 'You are too trusting, Watson. And a little naïve. Just because a fellow is a member of a gentleman's club does not mean that he is in fact a gentleman.'

'What are you suggesting?'

'I am wondering if we were lured here. That your "gentleman" gained your friendship and confidence in order to make sure that you brought me to this isolated cottage.'

'That's preposterous.'

'Maybe, but equally it is also possible. After all the arrangements were made, did you encounter the fellow at your club?'

I thought for a moment. 'No,' I said slowly. 'As a matter of fact I didn't.'

'The possible becomes probable,' observed Holmes brightly.

'But are you saying that there was some elaborate scheme to bring you to this cottage in order to play games with disappearing dead bodies?'

'Well, there must be some method in their madness.'

'Who are they?'

'Time will reveal all. But now we have a certain fellow to convey to the police station in Totnes. Will you get the horse between the shafts and bring the cart around to the front of the cottage? I'll prepare our passenger for his journey.'

The horse was stabled in a small outbuilding at the back of the cottage. Shrugging on my overcoat, I made my way there and to my dismay I saw that the door was open, the bolt having been released. I stood on the threshold and peered into the darkness of the interior. As I did so, I sensed movement behind me but before I was able to turn around, I felt a sharp, fierce pain at the back of my head. My brain seemed to explode and just as I realised that I was falling to the ground, I lost consciousness.

Eight

Composed from Notes made by Dr Watson

Sherlock Holmes had donned his ulster and carried the body of the Reverend Dickens into the sitting room in readiness to convey him out to the cart when Watson eventually arrived with the vehicle at the front door. Holmes waited some ten minutes but Watson did not appear. At first, it was frustration that governed the detective's emotions, but then a little dark stain of concern and unease began to grow in the corner of his mind. With some apprehension, he left the cottage and hurried around to the outbuilding at the rear. The door was open but there was no sign of his friend. He called out Watson's name but there was no response. Retrieving his revolver from his coat pocket, he ventured inside. As he did so the door was slammed shut behind him and he heard the shooting of the bolt.

He threw his weight against the door but it was too late. It was firmly secured. He cursed silently at his own incompetence at being trapped so easily. He gazed around in the darkness, illuminated only by the thin strips of light that squeezed their way through the gaps in the timbers. The horse stood like an anthracite statue in the deep gloom, breathing gently, unmoved by the dramatic events that were taking place around him. Where, thought Holmes, was Watson? As he moved around the stable, he spied a rusty spade half concealed by the straw that littered the floor. Slipping his revolver back into his pocket, he grabbed the spade and attacked the door with the metal blade. He brought it down with great force and the ancient timbers responded by cracking and splitting. Holmes grinned darkly and attacked the door again. This time the blade crashed through the wood and, with splinters flying, a shaft of daylight streamed in. Two more assaults and there was a big enough aperture in the door for Holmes to peer out.

All was quiet. The air was still and there was no one to be seen. Whoever had trapped him in the hut had gone or was in hiding. Slipping his arm through the jagged opening, Sherlock Holmes managed to reach the bolt and withdraw it, thus releasing himself from his temporary prison. He pushed the door wide and stepped out into the fresh air. Apart from the faint rustle of the wind through the dry grasses and the occasional cry of a seabird, there was no sound at all.

On instinct, he hurried around the building and into the cottage. It was as he suspected: the body of the Reverend Dickens had disappeared once again. Holmes couldn't help but smile at this bizarre game they were playing. Like mischievous children his enemies were carrying out a grotesque version of hide and seek. But what frustrated the sleuth was the fact that he had no clear notion what was behind this charade or what they expected to gain by their gruesome antics.

And where was Watson? This thought suddenly flashed in his mind and his body tensed with concern. What had happened to his friend? With a frenzied desperation, Holmes raced from room to room in the hope that he would discover his old companion. But the cottage was empty. That could only mean one thing.

They had Watson.

At least he was sure they hadn't killed him. For the moment.

Well, he thought, he would have to play their game for a while, if only for Watson's sake.

Within ten minutes, Sherlock Holmes was on the cart travelling along the dusty road towards Howden. It was a cloudy, sunless day and the grey cheerless sky seemed to press down heavily on the gently undulating countryside. There was no other soul in view and for all intents and purposes he could have been the last man on earth.

As he turned into the main street of the village it was just approaching noon, and the scene that was presented to him was as it had been the previous day: the street was silent and empty, nothing moved; not even the wind seemed to stir the trees.

He drove to the inn, tied the horse up and made his way to the entrance. On this occasion there were no men outside and in fact the door of the hostelry was closed. Holmes turned the handle and pushed the door open. He entered the sepulchral bar parlour which, like the street, was deserted. Holmes leaned on the bar and waited a few moments, tapping his fingers in a staccato rhythm on the counter. He was confident that his presence would have been noted. After all, he was the main actor in this bizarre and dangerous pantomime.

But no one came.

Eventually he called out. 'Good day, landlord.' His words echoed hollowly around the empty unlit bar but still no one appeared in response to his call. The place was truly deserted.

Holmes made his way behind the bar counter into the small room beyond which served as cramped living quarters. A fire crackled in the grate and a half-drunk mug of tea was set upon the table. Holmes touched its side. It was still warm.

He called out again although he knew it was a fruitless gesture. He searched the stockroom beyond and the rooms upstairs but there was no one there.

From the window he gazed down at the street and caught a glimpse of a dark figure hurrying towards the church. He could not make out whether it was a man or a woman for it wore a long gown, rather like a monk's habit, with a cowl over its head. The figure travelled with such speed that it appeared rather like a moving blur.

Holmes knew it was a sign. He was meant to see that figure. It was bait on their line drawing him in. Despite the implicit danger, he knew he could not ignore their 'invitation' – not if he wanted to see Watson alive again. Without hesitation, he left the inn and made his way towards the church. As he passed through the lychgate he thought he could hear singing, voices raised in some discordant chant. It was coming from within the church itself. His hand felt for the reassuring butt of his revolver as he approached the church door.

The singing grew louder.

His hand fell upon the great handle and turned it.

The door swung open with ease and Sherlock Holmes stepped inside.

Part Two

From Dr Watson's Journal

'Will this rain never stop,' I groaned as I stared out of the window of our Baker Street rooms at the flurry of umbrellas bouncing along the pavement below. The panes were bleared by the torrential rain and they rattled in their sockets as the wind buffeted our building. This was the third day of the unceasing downpour, and not only did it depress the spirits but also the dampness aggravated my old war wound and brought me a great deal of discomfort.

Holmes was curled up on the chaise longue by the fire in his purple dressing gown like a large contented cat. Puffing away on his church warden pipe, he was deep in some esoteric text about the Monmouth rebellion as he had been for some days, and had hardly noticed the inclement conditions outside. When clients were thin on the ground, he often chose to research a subject of which he knew little in order to keep his mind active. As he approached the age of fifty he relied less and less on drugs to stimulate him. I believed that he had indulged himself so frequently in his younger days that cocaine, whatever percentage the solution was, worked less effectively on his brain cells than it had once done. Habit had reduced the opiate's efficacy. Tackling arcane topics was now more stimulating to his tired brain.

He made a muttered indistinct response to my bleat about the weather, then after a few moments he turned as though struck by a sudden thought and addressed me. 'Oh, do take a seat, Watson. Pacing up and down will not change circumstances. Treat yourself to a glass of Beaune. You know how that eases the old injury. I've noticed your wound has been troubling you somewhat and I really don't think you have fully recovered from your recent illness.'

Before I could reply there was a jangle at the bell downstairs.

'A client.' Holmes raised his eyebrow in gentle query. I glanced down into the street below and saw that an individual was perched on our threshold, although his identity was masked by a large umbrella. He was admitted by Billy the page and moments later there was a soft rapping at our door.

Holmes threw me a glance of smug anticipation and bade our visitor enter. With some force a tall young man bustled into the room. Obviously Billy had relieved him of his outer coat but he still carried his dripping umbrella.

'Good day,' he said in a stilted fashion and seemed to regard me somewhat furtively. There was something about the fellow that was familiar. I seemed to know that face and the voice. I felt as though I had met him before but I could not recall where or when. This was probably due to my recent illness, from which I believe I had recovered quite effectively in a physical sense, but I still suffered from memory loss. The events leading up to my hospitalisation were a complete blank to me. Try as I might, my mind refused to conjure up the details. I had to rely on Holmes' account of my decline. It had never been clearly diagnosed what had brought about the fever which had led me down the hellish path of hallucinations and terrifying dreams. As I understood it, I had almost become a candidate for Bedlam. Although he would not admit it to me, I knew that it was Holmes' loyalty and perseverance that had secured the best medical attention possible. With careful nursing, I was weaned away from my wild and dark visions and my grip on reality had gradually strengthened once more. I was still not quite myself and I longed for Holmes to have a challenging and intriguing case so that I was forced to gird up my loins and become a practical fellow once more, rather than sitting around our Baker Street rooms twiddling my thumbs. Maybe this visitor was the very person to instigate such a scenario.

'My dear fellow,' Holmes was saying to the young man, 'come, take a chair by the fire and make yourself warm.'

'Thank you, sir,' said the visitor, still casting unnerving glances in my direction.

'Watson, old fellow, would you be so kind as to ask Mrs Hudson to make some tea? I trust that would be acceptable?' He addressed this last remark to our visitor, who was now ensconced in the wicker chair by the fire.

He nodded. 'Indeed, refreshment would be most welcome. I've… I've had rather a long journey.'

Holmes smiled and cast a glance in my direction as though to prompt my actions. This was most unlike him, treating me as though I were his manservant, but I did as he bade me.

Mrs Hudson was in the middle of a baking session when I knocked gently and entered her domestic domain.

'If you'll give me a moment to get these cakes in the oven, then I'll organise the tea,' she said in response to my request. 'Sit yourself down and I'll not be long.'

Mrs Hudson had a way with her, gentle, kindly, while at the same time commanding, so that one tended to do as she asked without demur, and so I sat down in her warm kitchen while she busied herself with her baking.

'Mr Holmes has a client, I take it? I heard the bell,' she said, rinsing her hands under the tap.

'A visitor at least. Whether he turns out to be a client is another matter.'

She gave a little chuckle. 'Well let's hope so. I know he's been bored these last few weeks. He's never at his best when he's nothing to occupy his mind.'

I nodded in agreement. The topic of Holmes' irritability and the various manifestations of his frustrated boredom when he had no investigation to occupy his mind was a familiar one to us both.

'I worry about him, you know, Doctor. He has not been himself for some time now. I fully expected that break by the sea would have refreshed him but it doesn't seem to have. Certainly, it laid you low, Doctor. Did they ever get to the bottom of what you had?'

'I'm afraid not. It was all so mysterious. I feel rather foolish really. I should be able to heal myself, or at least diagnose what was wrong with me.'

'Life is strange like that. Don't you fuss. At least you're back to your old self again.'

I nodded and smiled. I didn't want to admit that I felt far from being my old self again. I still suffered from bouts of fatigue and my memory of my time with Holmes on the coast was shot to pieces. And there were those dark nightmares that still visited me. I was only able to escape from their terrifying clutches by the cry of terror that shook me awake, dragging me back to reality where I found myself dripping with sweat and shivering with fear without being able to determine the cause. On such occasions, I spent the rest of the night with the candle lit by my bed.

The kettle boiled and with dexterous efficiency Mrs Hudson

prepared a tray with teapot, milk, sugar, crockery and a plate of her oatmeal biscuits.

When I returned to the sitting room bearing the tray, I found that Sherlock Holmes was the sole occupant. He was standing at the window, staring out at the rain-sodden street, but there was no sign of our visitor.

'Ah, tea. Excellent!' observed Holmes, turning to face me, his stern features breaking briefly into a smile.

'Where is the young man?' I asked.

'He has gone. It was a trifling matter. Not worth my attention. I sent him on his way. I am a detective, not a nanny or an agent for discovering lost spectacles, missing library books and other such inconsequential matters.' There was irritation in his voice but it was not genuine. He was lying to me.

'What exactly was the nature of his problem?'

Holmes gave an exclamation of displeasure. 'I shall waste neither my time and energy, nor your patience, by discussing the matter. Be a good fellow and pour the tea and let's turn our minds to more important matters.'

I did as he asked, but I was far from satisfied. I was convinced that my friend was covering something up. His overdramatic prickly reaction concerning the would-be client was unconvincing to me, a close companion who had known him and his moods and humours over a great number of years. I cannot deny that this not only irritated me but hurt me also. Holmes was not a man who kept secrets, at least not from me, his one true friend. As I sipped my tea I tried to persuade myself that Holmes must have a very good reason to behave as he did.

We fell into desultory conversation for a while and then he picked up his Stradivarius and began playing a series of melancholy airs. I returned to my reading but I was unable to concentrate as my mind wandered back to our visitor and Holmes' strange behaviour regarding him.

Daylight faltered with the onset of evening; the rain stopped and the wind ceased to rattle the panes of our rooms. As I lit the gas my friend roused himself, flinging off his dressing gown as he shrugged on his frock coat.

'I feel the need for some air, Watson, and I'm running low on tobacco, so I'll take myself out for a stroll and call at Bradley's on the way to buy a fresh stock. I won't be long, old fellow.'

I rose from my chair. 'Exercise will do me good. I'll come along with you.'

Holmes shook his head. 'I want solitude, not conversation, or even a silent fellow trotting by my side. You are an ideal companion, Watson, but at times, as I'm sure you know, I prefer my own company.'

It was true but he had never expressed the thought so brutally before. I looked at my friend with fresh eyes. Was this the Sherlock Holmes of old? Well, the face was more careworn and lined. The eyes were still as sharp and penetrating as ever. But, I had to admit, there was a kind of coldness and oddness about his behaviour that was alien to him. I knew that he had struggled with some demons and that was why I had arranged for us to have that holiday on the coast in… in… for the life of me I was unable to recall the location. Everything about that trip was a grey void in my mind. That was the remnants of my brain fever. Maybe… maybe something had happened on that vacation which had helped to bring about this subtle and yet radical change in my friend's demeanour. I just could not remember. I had searched in vain for my journal covering this period in the hope that it would provide me with the information I required, or at least some clues as to what really happened but I could not find it. It seemed to have disappeared. Thus that time of my life remained a blank in my mind.

Holmes donned his hat and extricated his cane from the base of the hat rack.

'I will see you later,' he said before making a swift exit.

I spent little time in deciding what to do. A few seconds only. I sprang from my chair and grabbed my coat. I would follow him. If he was just going for a stroll, calling in at Bradley's during his perambulations, then no harm was done. However, if he was going elsewhere, somewhere with a purpose that he wished to hide from me, then it could lead me to an explanation as to why my friend was behaving so oddly.

As I slipped out of 221B onto the street, I espied Holmes about a hundred yards ahead of me. He was walking briskly and with purpose, and heading in the opposite direction to Bradley's the tobacconist.

I felt an uneasy tingle down my spine as I set off in pursuit.

Ten

From Dr Watson's Journal

Luck was on my side, for not only had I a moonless night to assist me in shadowing my friend Sherlock Holmes, but after the rain a fine mist netted the air, giving me further cover. As a result I was able to keep quite close to Holmes without him seeing me clearly. He seemed quite oblivious to my presence some thirty yards behind him. Indeed, he was walking with such a purposeful tread, his head bent forward, zigzagging with consummate skill through the throng of pedestrians who crowded the pavements, that he appeared not to notice anyone or anything of his surroundings.

On reaching the end of Baker Street, he hailed a cab. I moved as close to him as I dared in order to hear his instructions to the cabby. He gave an address in Houndsditch which I committed to memory. With a lash of the whip, the cab was off at a fast pace. Luckily, I was able to secure a second hansom before Holmes was out of sight. I gave the cabby the same address with the promise of a bonus coin if he could get me there in a hurry.

His grimy face broke into a grin. 'It's what I do naturally,' he said, 'but a little extra cash always ensures satisfaction.'

With that he roused his steed and we rattled off into the night.

Houndsditch is one of the less salubrious areas of London. It is an unkempt thoroughfare that connects Bishopsgate in the north-west to Aldgate in the south-east. It is not a stone's throw from Whitechapel, the scene of the horrific Ripper murders some dozen years before. Houndsditch marks the route of the ancient ditch running outside a section of the old London Wall. The name 'Houndsditche' first appeared in the thirteenth century relating to the quantity of rubbish and dead dogs thrown in the ditch. In a similar way, it is still a receptacle for the human debris that the city harbours in its darker quarters. It is the habitat of thieves, prostitutes and worse. One could only assume that Holmes was visiting this place because of some investigation he was engaged upon – one of which he had, for whatever reason, denied me knowledge.

We made excellent time and although I had lost sight of Holmes' cab, I was sure that he could not be far ahead of me. As we turned from Bishopsgate into Houndsditch, I asked my eager driver to halt and after paying him generously for his efforts, I alighted and made my way down the murky thoroughfare.

Suddenly the night seemed darker and colder and the air polluted with a faint acrid smell. I wondered if this was simply my fancy because I was in such dreary and inhospitable surroundings. It always surprised me that this great city with its fine buildings and majestic avenues could still harbour such decrepit and desolate areas as this, like unsightly growths marring a fine complexion. The street was quiet, but a few stray ragged phantoms drifted by me. Occasionally their grey faces were caught by the feeble amber flare from the odd drunken-looking gas lamp, leering at me with undisguised suspicion. My smart clothes easily marked me out as an alien in that environment.

Some way ahead of me on the other side of the street, I spied another cab. It was just turning round and departing, leaving its solitary passenger standing pensively on the kerb. I instantly recognised that tall, spare silhouette.

It was Sherlock Holmes.

I felt a rush of excitement. I had actually managed to track down my friend without him being aware of the fact. I pulled myself back against the wall into the gloom and observed him. He stood stiffly, gazing around him as though he did not know what to do or which direction to take. It was possible, I conjectured, that he was waiting for someone: this was to be a rendezvous.

Keeping to the shadows, I edged closer to him. And then suddenly out of nowhere it seemed there was another figure in the dreary landscape. It emerged out of the blackness as though by magic. It was a man of approximately the same size and build as Holmes. He approached my friend with a swift deliberation that quickened my senses. The two men indulged in a hurried conversation. Their voices were low and I was too far away to catch anything that passed between then. And then with a shocking suddenness, the man stepped back from Holmes and, withdrawing a stick from the folds of his coat, brought it down on my friend's head. Holmes staggered back but remained upright. It was clear that the attack had caught him completely by surprise. As he teetered in a dazed state, his assailant brought the stick down upon his head once more. This time Holmes crumpled to the ground.

'Stop!' I cried, as I rushed towards the terrible tableau: my friend lying prone on the damp pavement while his attacker stood over him brandishing the cane high above his head. At the sound of my voice the assailant froze, and then with a sharp snap of the head glanced in my direction. On spying me, the coward wasted no time and took to his heels, running like the devil. I chased him some twenty yards but he was fleet of foot and very quickly the curtain of night shielded him from my view. Reluctantly, I gave up the chase and returned to Holmes, who was still lying on the pavement groaning.

Feeling inside my coat and retrieving my brandy flask, I knelt down and cradled his head in my arms as I placed the open flask at his lips. It was then that I had the shock of my life. The wounded man was not Sherlock Holmes. It was someone I had never seen before.

His eyes opened lazily and he took a sip of brandy. Then suddenly, without any warning, I found the fellow's hands around my throat. With great force, he pulled me over onto the ground so that our positions were reversed. I now lay on my back with the brute towering over me, his bulk holding me pressed to the ground while his large coarse fingers began throttling the life out of me. Such was the shock of this dramatic turn of events that it took me some moments before I was able to retaliate. I pushed hard against the brute, humping my body violently, my legs giving me some purchase to thrust the fellow from me. But it was to no avail. He retained the fierce grip on my throat, squeezing the air out of me. My mind began to fog and I became aware that my struggles were diminishing as a dark, drowsy numbness overtook me. My hands reached out in desperation to thrust the fiend away but by now they had lost power and flapped helplessly as I slipped into the ebony void of unconsciousness.

How long I drowned in that black sea I don't know, but gradually I began to surface and eventually I became aware of a general ache. It was as though my body had been placed in a giant vice which was slowly being pressed shut. At length, I felt able to open my eyes. They flickered erratically and then attempted to focus. I tried to make sense of my surroundings. Slowly, my brain sought explanations and memory. My body was twisted in an awkward position and I realised that I was lying on the ground, the hard damp ground. Slowly, I became conscious of the pain at my throat and my fingers sought it out and touched it gingerly. Then it came back to me. The moments leading up to my decline. I shook my head in an attempt to dispel the fog inside. I saw again my assailant louring over me and his hard fingers at my throat. I shuddered at the vision. Well, I thought, with more than a bitter chagrin, at least the fellow didn't kill me – unless I am in hell.

With some effort I pulled myself up onto my elbow and tried to identify where I really was and establish that I was not in fact in the nether regions. Remarkably I discovered that I was lying exactly where I had fallen when I'd been attacked. A bleak moonless sky seemed to press down upon me. Suddenly, a rat scurried over my legs causing me to groan with disgust and jerk myself up into an upright posture, an action that set off a series of minor explosions in my brain. With gritted teeth, I glanced around me. Apart from the rodent, I was alone again. With some effort, I dragged myself to my feet and stood, swaying unsteadily for some moments while I tried to establish my equilibrium once more. I felt inside my coat pocket and discovered that my wallet had gone, along with my watch and chain. I groaned with dismay. I had been thoroughly humiliated. Not only had I been duped but robbed into the bargain. My aching brain told me that I needed to return home and rest. Certainly there was no trail here to follow. What had happened to Sherlock Holmes and who the fellow was who had tried to strangle me was a mystery – a mystery I certainly was not going to solve this night. Luckily the blackguard who attacked me had not rifled my trouser pockets and I had enough loose change to pay for a cab back to Baker Street. Wearily and with some discomfort, I shambled down the ill-lit road towards one of the major thoroughfares in the hope of securing a hansom cab.

In just under an hour I was mounting those familiar seventeen steps up to our sitting room. My brain was clear but my body ached and my neck felt sore. I gave myself a wry grin. I was a wreck of a man. I had set out earlier that evening with confidence and good expectations, and now I returned wounded and none the wiser.

I entered the sitting room and found it in darkness apart from the dim rosy glow from the dying embers of the fire. There was no sign of Holmes. I poured myself a large brandy and downed it in one gulp. My sore throat throbbed painfully as the fierce alcohol burned its way down my oesophagus and I gasped in pain.

Like a man in a dream I retired to my room, flung off my clothes, dragged on my nightgown and sank into my bed, confused, and both mentally and physically exhausted.

Eleven

From Dr Watson's Journal

I will never know what propelled me into wakefulness before daylight had made its presence felt in the sky above London. It could have been the general ache I felt in my bones that constantly brought me into semi-consciousness whenever I shifted position under the covers; or it could have been the more specific discomfort in my throat – it felt as though it were on fire. However, I tend to think that it was the strange unintelligible sounds that insinuated themselves in my ear. Eventually, I gave up trying to sleep and sat up in bed attempting to shake the lethargy from my mind and body. I strained to identify the unusual droning noise that existed just on the edge of apprehension. Was this strange buzzing in my head or was it something else?

It was something else.

Wrapping my dressing gown around me I ventured out of my room and onto the landing. Now the sound was more distinct. It was like a muted conversation. Still feeling drugged by sleep, I crept warily towards the sitting room and paused outside the door, which was slightly ajar. Cautiously I nudged it open another inch and peered through the crack.

The chamber was in darkness apart from one flickering candle placed on the table by the window. Seated at the table were two men facing each other in a conspiratorial manner, engaged in earnest and whispered conversation. One of the men was Sherlock Holmes. The other was a stranger to me. Like my friend he was tall and gaunt, a skeleton of a man, and as he leaned forward towards the candle I could see that his ancient face was scarred and disfigured. Nonetheless, his eyes glittered brightly with animation and passion. Suddenly his bony arms reached across the table and he took hold of both of Holmes' hands. Raising his voice he uttered what seemed to be some kind of oath or incantation. It was in a language that was unknown to me. My friend responded in a similar fashion and then with an emotive sigh he threw his head back, his body rippling as though caught by some involuntary palsied spasm. All the while the candle flickered erratically, sending the shadows of the two men dancing wildly around the walls of the room. I was held mesmerised by this bizarre and strangely frightening scene.

Silence followed for some moments and then the muted conversation between the two men began again. I was tempted to rush into the room and demand to know what on earth was going on, but after my experiences of the previous evening I knew that caution and discretion were the essential requisites for the moment – until I could discover the nature of this baffling business in which my friend was involved.

As I stared into the darkness at this strange candlelit tableau, I suddenly felt an overwhelming sense of tiredness. My eyelids dropped and my legs grew almost too weary to bear my weight. Without a further thought, I staggered back to my bed where, on hitting the pillow, I was swallowed up by the deepest of sleeps.

When I eventually awoke, daylight was streaming into the room. I reached over to the bedside cabinet and retrieved my pocket watch. It was a quarter to noon. I had been asleep for nearly eight hours. As full consciousness came to me, I was reminded of the pain in my throat and gagged a little. I poured myself a glass of water to lubricate it. I gazed at my reflection in the dressing table mirror and sure enough there was a set of dark red blotches around my neck where the assailant's fingers had found strong and rough purchase. It was tender to the touch.

As I dressed I contemplated the events of the last twenty-four hours and wondered if I were living in a dream. Was I really having hallucinations? Was I in fact still suffering from the after effects of my recent strange illness? Was I going mad?

On entering the sitting room, I saw a note from Holmes propped on the mantelshelf. It read: 'Gone to visit Mycroft. Will not be back until late this evening. SH.'

I rang down for some hot tea with honey to soothe my throat and then tried to work out how I could solve this mystery. At the best of times, I was intellectually in the shadow of my brilliant friend, but these were not the best of times. I felt old, weary and more than usually confused by events. I had been taken out of the arena of reality and cast adrift. In this instance Holmes couldn't help me – he was part of my problem – and my mind and memory were ragged and out of focus. I felt sure the key to my dilemma lay in the time Holmes and I had spent by the coast – his supposedly relaxing holiday. The one that Cawthorne had recommended…

I stopped, my heart thumping violently. Where had that name and thought come from? I had until this very moment completely forgotten about Cawthorne and his blasted cottage. And now the memory had been vouchsafed me. With my head in my hands I concentrated on the fellow's name, and slowly and in a ragged fashion the facts gradually filtered back to me. In a vague vision I saw him, a small red-faced man, Pickwickian in build and demeanour. I recalled how charming he had been to me, how amenable and deprecating. He was a regular and gracious loser to me at the billiard table. I could see now that occasions when he lost a game by a careless move or incompetent judgement were too frequent to be natural. It was as though he had let me win to buoy up my confidence, to simply please me, to win my trust and secure my compliance. He had succeeded. At this distance and viewed with a dispassionate curiosity, I began to see that the fellow had targeted me for friendship. Strangely, I felt unnerved by this revelation for I not only believed that it was significant but, without knowing why, I was convinced that it was the first key piece in the dark and enigmatic puzzle that I had to unravel.

While I was not sure exactly in what way I had made some progress with this revelation, it did give me the basis on which I could formulate a rough plan of action. I contemplated this further while I drank my tea. This honeyed brew did much to ease my throat and helped me focus on the problem at hand. Settled on my plan, with a jaunty resolve, I donned my outer clothing and set forth from Baker Street on my investigations.

'Great heavens, Watson, where did you spring from?' My friend Joe Thurston jumped from his chair, rounded his desk and, stepping forward, clasped my hand in his with great enthusiasm. 'You are a sight for sore eyes, I can tell you,' he beamed.

Such a genuine and warm-hearted greeting was good for my soul and for an instant my spirits soared. Apart from Holmes, he was the only true friend I had in London, but to be frank our friendship was of a casual nature which had developed in a casual fashion over the years always within the confines of my club. There we were billiard partners and drinking companions. To my recollection I had never seen him outside the walls of that establishment. Therefore he must have been doubly astonished to see me walk into his small office at the firm of solicitors where he was a senior partner.

'Take a seat, old fellow, and tell me what brings you here. I haven't seen you in a while. I had heard you'd been in the wars… and I must say you are not looking your usual perky self.'

I grinned. With Joe Thurston honesty always took pride of place over discretion. I suppose that was one reason why I liked and trusted the man. He was tall and stoutish and although a few years younger than me, his rosy-cheeked face was topped with a mop of thick grey hair.

'I need your help, Joe,' I said simply, taking a chair opposite his desk, the client's chair no doubt. I thought this was appropriate because in a sense I was a client now. In some detail – as much as I could remember – I told him my tale. I remembered virtually nothing about the holiday on the coast, but I had recalled Cawthorne and his suggestion of renting a cottage he had used and I was able to recount in great detail the events of the previous evening.

Thurston sat in rapt attention throughout my narration, his bright eyes twinkling with interest and concern.

'Well,' he said when I had finished, 'that's quite a story and quite a problem. You are sure that you should not simply confront Holmes with your concerns as you have done with me?'

I shook my head vigorously. 'No, it is clear that he is deliberately hiding something from me. He is well practised at subterfuge but I know his ways. I would get nowhere approaching him. I have to find out for myself.'

Thurston nodded sagely. 'I understand. But where do I come in?'

I allowed myself a sly smile. 'I need an accomplice. A partner in my investigations.'

Thurston laughed out loud. 'You mean you want me to turn detective,' he said, grinning. His demeanour indicated that he found the whole idea highly amusing and fanciful, but there was a glint in his eyes which told a slightly different story. They widened with excitement.

'I need a companion I can trust. This is not a job for a solitary investigator.'

Thurston's attitude sobered. 'Well, if you put it like that... I must confess I have always felt a pang of jealousy when you have recounted your various investigative exploits with Sherlock Holmes. Now you are asking me to join in on the game.'

'Yes, but I suspect you will find it more dangerous than a game. Are you up for it?'

Thurston did not reply at first. He rose from his chair and wandered to the window, where he absent-mindedly pulled back the net curtain a few inches to peer out into the street beyond. Suddenly he turned to me, his features taut and serious.

'So, friend Watson, what do you want me to do?'

Twelve

From Dr Watson's Journal

The Army and Navy Club, an impressive Portland stone edifice, is situated in Pall Mall on the corner of George Street. I had been a member there since I returned from serving as an army surgeon in Afghanistan. Thurston, too, had seen action as a captain in that hot and perilous locale, although our paths had never crossed out there. We approached the building as Big Ben was striking the hour, our plan of action firmly fixed in our minds.

Our first task was a simple one. As we signed ourselves in, we riffled through the pages of the sturdy ledger to find the last time Cawthorne had been in the club. It took us some time to locate the crabbed scrawl that passed for the fellow's signature. I looked at the date. It was nearly two months before. Around the time I had left on holiday with Holmes. The facts seemed clear to me.

'After he had achieved his goal, he had no further use for the club,' I explained to Thurston, returning the pages of the book to the current date.

'And that goal was to persuade you to take residence in Devon at Samphire Cottage.'

I nodded. 'Indeed.'

Our second task was more complicated and required a certain amount of subterfuge and nerve. I needed to see the secretary's book in which he recorded the members' personal details, including their addresses. This leather-bound volume sat in pride of place on the desk in his office, which was situated just off the foyer. When he was not in his office, the chamber was locked. The secretary was Colonel Sir James Warburton, who, having retired from the army many years ago, had brought his military precision and order to his role in the club. He certainly would not willingly reveal any personal details regarding another member and it would be difficult to gain access to the book without his knowledge.

But Thurston and I had a plan.

Some moments later I was making my way to the rear of the building where there was a small lawned area. Warburton's office was on the ground floor with a view of this small stretch of greenery. I located his window with little difficulty and with great care peered in. I could see Warburton sitting at his desk, his back towards me, smoking a cigar and poring over some documents on his desk. By his right hand was the membership ledger.

I had not to wait long before I heard a muffled knock at the door and Warburton's curt stentorian response of 'Enter'. The door of the room opened and my colleague, Joe Thurston, entered. The alacrity and enthusiasm with which Joe had fallen in with my plans had been most surprising. Without hesitation, he had cancelled all his appointments for the rest of the day and informed his secretary that he might be absent until further notice. 'There, Watson,' he'd announced cheerfully as we left his chambers, 'I'm yours to do your bidding. Let's solve this mystery.'

It had been arranged that Joe would seek an audience with the secretary and present him with a faulty bar bill – one that we had carefully doctored to make it look as though Joe had been grossly overcharged. It was a common fault at the club and was not likely to raise any undue suspicion.

I could see from Joe's facial expression and demeanour that he was only just suppressing his excitement in enacting this charade. I could not hear the conversation between the two men but it was rather like watching an expert dumb show and having some knowledge of the plot; I could tell what was happening. Thurston wandered up and down the room, apparently expressing various pleasantries before getting to the nub of his visit. Casually he strolled to the window, making some comment about the garden beyond. At this I dropped down out of sight, but I did hear the catch on the window frame being moved.

When I looked again, Thurston was sitting in a chair opposite the colonel's desk and brandishing the forged bar bill, which he passed to Warburton for his scrutiny. The colonel slipped his pince-nez firmly on his nose and examined the slip of paper. Thurston kept up a stream of dialogue, punctuated by questions and small exclamations. I could see that this was a ruse to interfere with the colonel's concentration.

At length the colonel rose from his chair and indicated the door. Surely he wasn't dismissing my friend. But no, he was accompanying him. They were going to investigate the matter further – probably by visiting the bar and checking the accounts. As soon as they had left the room, I was able to heave up the window so cunningly released by my partner in crime and clamber inside.

It did not take me long to search through the membership book and find the entry for Edric Cawthorne. Quickly, I made a note of his address on my cuff, a habit I had picked up from Holmes, and then exited the room at great speed the same way I'd entered, closing the window as I did so. I now made my way around to the front entrance and took a seat in the foyer and waited for Thurston to appear. When he did so, he looked a little perturbed. 'I think I've blotted my copybook with old Warburton,' were his first words.

'He didn't believe you?'

'Well, he did not say as much outright, but he eyed me most suspiciously. He's too much of a gentleman to question my veracity, but let's say that he probably thinks I'm a cheat or charlatan, or worst of all, not much of a gentleman.'

He grinned and then chuckled and I must admit I joined in the laughter, too.

'And were you successful?' Thurston asked when he had mastered his emotions.

I nodded and held up my cuff for his examination. 'I got the address,' I said.

'Then what are we waiting for?' he said eagerly, pulling me to my feet.

The address that I had noted down from the ledger was in Balfour Mews in Paddington. Our cab dropped us a few streets away. We wanted to approach the property on foot and spy on it surreptitiously. We negotiated the intervening streets and within five minutes we were walking down Balfour Mews in a casual fashion, affecting an amiable conversation while our eyes keenly scrutinised the area. When we arrived at the address that Cawthorne had given, my heart sank. The property seemed shabby and run down and by the look of the dirty blank boarded windows that stared at us as we passed, it was uninhabited.

'Not the town house of a gentleman,' observed Thurston wryly as we sauntered by.

'Nevertheless, let's try the door,' I said. We passed through the gate and down a short path. I thumped the knocker loudly several times. We could hear it booming inside the building but there was no reply. I tried the door handle but it was firmly secure.

'This has been a wild goose chase, old boy,' said Thurston, trying to peer through the cracks of the boarded dirt-smeared bow window. 'No one has lived here for quite a while. It seems that Cawthorne gave a false address.'

I nodded in agreement. 'Most likely, but we need to look at the rear of the building,' I said. 'Appearances are sometimes deceptive. It would be useful if we could gain entrance and have a scout around inside at least.'

'Anything you say,' grinned my companion.

We sauntered to the end of the mews and found our way back down a narrow lane, unpaved and muddy, that ran along the rear of the houses. Having located the right property we made our way up a narrow overgrown garden to the back door. This was similarly secured but the window to the left of it had not been boarded up. I explained to Thurston that we must break the window and thereby gain entrance to the house.

He looked doubtful. 'I think it's a bit pointless, Watson. No one can be living here, and certainly not Cawthorne.'

In my heart I had to agree with him, but I was imbued with the tenacity I had developed after many years of associating with Holmes. When he was on the scent he was like a bloodhound, not easily deterred or dismayed. Also at the back of my mind was the thought that while this was obviously not Cawthorne's residence, he had, in some way, to know of this address and therefore it was some link, however tenuous, with him.

I was just about to let Thurston off the hook and allow him to bow out while I continued when something extraordinary caught my eye. The house was a narrow three-storey one, and at one of the windows on the second floor I momentarily saw a light, as though someone with a candle or oil lamp had just passed by it.

Excitedly I conveyed this information to my friend. He seemed unimpressed. 'Are you sure?' he asked, as though he was convinced that I was mistaken. 'A trick of the light surely. Who would be carrying a lamp in this mouldy old property, and up there?'

Strangely he pointed to the exact window where I had seen the light. I had not indicated this fact to him.

'Are you sure you didn't see it also?' I asked somewhat petulantly.

Thurston shook his head. 'No. But... if you are determined to go ahead, I won't let you down. Go ahead – break the window.'

I gave a taut smile and nodded. Using the head of my cane I fractured the window pane as quietly as I could. Gradually I knocked out all the glass, so that we could slip through the aperture without cutting our gloves or snagging our coats.

In less than five minutes we had both clambered into the dank-smelling house. We stood for a moment in what was a kind of kitchen area – there was a sink and a primitive oven – and listened. All I could hear was the strange hissing silence and the lazy scampering of rodent life.

'Let's make our way upstairs,' I said in a harsh whisper. The light was failing and I cursed myself that I had not brought a dark lantern to help illuminate our passage.

We moved into the hallway and then began to climb the stairs. The property was unfurnished and reeked of damp and decay. I was beginning to feel, like Thurston, that this was a wild goose chase. I had been wrong. Cawthorne must have just plucked this address at random and had no real connection with the property whatsoever. On reaching the first landing, I glanced into the few bedrooms but they were empty. There was not a stick of furniture or any item that indicated that these rooms had been lived in.

However, as we moved up towards the second landing, there was a definite change in the atmosphere. The place seemed warmer for a start, and the smell of damp and decay had filtered away. Was that a smell of food that I caught in the air? As we reached the second-floor landing, I was aware of carpet beneath my feet and at the end of the corridor, set upon a small polished table, was an oil lamp flickering in the gloom. My eyes widened with pleasure and surprise. This was no deserted town house. Here were signs of habitation.

It seemed to me that the outer appearance of the building and the dilapidation of the lower floors were a cover, a false front designed to deceive. I was just about to turn and convey this observation to my friend when I received a blow to the back of the head delivered with such force that I lost consciousness before my body hit the floor.

Thirteen

ᏋᎦ

From Dr Watson's Journal

I was dragged back into consciousness by someone shaking my shoulders and calling my name. Slowly I opened my eyes to see the gaunt features of a ragged individual who was leaning over me, grasping my shoulders in a rough attempt to rouse me. The tramp's long grey hair framed his grubby, unwashed and unshaven features, but his eyes were bright and intelligent. And it seemed to me, in my groggy state, he was concerned for my welfare.

'Back in the land of the living, eh, Watson?'

I knew that voice. I knew those eyes staring at me from that ruin of a face.

'Holmes!' I croaked and pulled myself into a sitting position.

'Yes. It's Holmes. And what a fine muddle you've got yourself into.'

'Muddle!' I cried indignantly, my mind clearing. I was about to open my mouth again in protest when I suddenly thought of Thurston.

'Where is Joe Thurston?'

Holmes nodded towards the far corner of the room. 'He's over there and still out. He received a blow to the back of the head also.'

'Who attacked us?'

'One of the coven. Luckily my sudden appearance frightened him off.'

'Coven? Holmes, what on earth is going on? What dark business are you mixed up in?'

'Yes, it is a dark and a very dangerous business, and your interfering has made it all the more dangerous.'

I shook my head and for a moment my sight became blurred. 'I don't know what you are talking about,' I said with some heat.

'I'm glad to hear it, and that's the way it must be.'

'Look,' I said, pulling myself up into a sitting position, 'I was nearly strangled last night and bashed on the head just now. It's a wonder I've still got a skull I can call my own. These attacks alone prove that I am in the thick of the action – whatever the action is – and so I deserve to know what in heaven's name is going on.'

Holmes pursed his lips and rolled his eyes towards the ceiling. 'If you had not tried to interfere, to pry where you should not, you would not have suffered any of the injuries or indignities. No doubt you attempted to follow me to Houndsditch last night?'

'Yes, I did.'

Holmes could not resist a sly grin. 'I thought you might. You heard me give the cabby those instructions?'

I nodded.

'But you didn't hear me give him a completely different destination once we were on the move.'

'What?'

'Whoever you encountered at Houndsditch had nothing to do with me. Some roughs playing one of their games with you. You are no doubt some pounds lighter in your wallet – if you still have your wallet. And I observe your watch and chain are missing.'

'They got them too.'

Holmes nodded gravely. 'Curiosity killed the cat, Watson. Stay out of this affair.'

'I have always shared your dangers. I have a right to know.'

'This case is very different, believe me. I assure you it is in your best interests – indeed your life depends upon it – that you do not know.'

'My life?'

'What you don't know cannot hurt you.'

I rubbed the back of my head. 'That theory does not seem to be working,' I observed wryly. Then the words struck me again. 'My *life*, you say?'

Holmes nodded.

'Great heavens!' I cried, as the full implications of my friend's statements dawned on me. 'You have been… protecting me.'

'In a way.'

'This has something to do with our time in Devon, hasn't it? At Samphire Cottage?'

Holmes did not reply but the slight flicker of his eyelids told me I was right.

'I have no memory of that time.'

'It has been wiped from your "trivial fond records".'

'Wiped?'

'It would be inconvenient for you to remember.'

Despite myself, I shook my head again. 'What do you mean? Inconvenient for whom?'

'You must trust me in this matter, Watson. You must stop your investigations and be satisfied to be kept in the dark for the moment.'

'If there is danger, I wish to share it with you.'

Holmes stifled a smile. 'You sound like the hero in one of those rousing adventure yarns you devour on rainy evenings. There is danger certainly, but it would grow tenfold if you were to continue your interfering.'

'Interfering!'

'What have your activities achieved? Bludgeoned twice and, I'm afraid to say, threatened not only your own safety but mine also. You must drop it, Watson. You really must.' He grabbed my arm with some urgency and added quietly, 'For both our sakes.'

Never had my friend made such an earnest and urgent entreaty to me. I felt cowed and penitent. 'What do you want me to do?' I asked.

'In simple terms: nothing. First of all, you must see to your associate over there. Rouse him gently and put him in a cab and send him home. Declare that the case is closed and you will not be requiring his services any further. Not a word to him about this interview, I beg you. Then I want you to go back to Baker Street and keep a low profile. I shall be away for a few days, maybe a week, and then hopefully on my return I will be able to explain everything.'

'Can't you at least give me some idea what this infernal business is all about?'

Holmes shook his head and his mouth tightened with exasperation. 'Haven't I made that abundantly clear to you? Now I must be away. I have stayed longer than I should. If they knew I'd been talking to you my life would not be worth a pin's fee. Or yours.'

With these words he drew back into the shadows and in a matter of seconds he had disappeared from the room.

I sat for some moments in the gloom, partly to allow myself time to summon enough energy to get to my feet and attend to Thurston and partly to try and make sense of the conversation that I'd just had with Holmes. The injunctions were forceful but the information he had supplied was scant in the extreme. I was no wiser as to the extent and nature of the danger that threatened us. I knew that it must be severe for Holmes to behave in this bizarre and mysterious way but I could not rationalise in my own head why he did not share this information with me. Why had I been deliberately kept ignorant of the true situation? If my life was at risk, surely Holmes should have told me the nature of the threat so that I could take appropriate precautions and not be left groping about in the dark. I felt as frustrated, confused and indeed angry as I had been before I had entered this house.

My ruminations were interrupted by a moan from the far corner and I saw that Thurston was awakening from his enforced slumbers. With groggy utterances, he pulled himself up into a sitting position, almost mirroring my pose in the opposite corner. As his eyes began to focus, he caught sight of me. 'Watson, by all that's wonderful. Are you all right?'

'Dented a little about the skull, but I will live,' I said. 'And you?'

He gave a grim smile and rubbed the back of his head. 'Much the same, I reckon.'

I dragged myself to my feet and with unsteady steps I went over to my friend. 'Come on, old boy, let me haul you up.' I extended my arms, which he grasped, and with some effort I managed to get him to his feet.

'That's better,' he said, without much conviction. And then he gave a little smile. 'This is a rum business, all right. You didn't warn me that I might get beaten about the head when I agreed to help you.'

'I'm sorry, Thurston. It came as a surprise to me also. If I'd known...'

My friend threw up his hand. 'Don't apologise, for goodness' sake. This has been the most exciting day I've had since I left the army. I can see why you're keen on this detective business. What's our next move?'

With great enthusiasm Thurston stepped forward and then awkwardly fell towards me. I caught his arm and supported him.

'Oh, the legs are still a bit wobbly,' he said, his voice suddenly weak.

I helped him over to a large tea chest near the grimy window and he perched on the edge of it, mopping his brow, his face damp with perspiration.

'Not... not as young as I was,' he muttered.

I examined the back of his head. The skin had not been broken but he possessed a fair-sized lump.

'We need to get you home. You need to rest. You're obviously suffering from mild concussion.'

Thurston turned to me as though he was about to reject my suggestion, but the sudden movement of his head caused him to flinch. 'Perhaps… perhaps you are right. But what about you?'

'I think I must do the same. I believe it's time to bring a halt to my investigations for a while and wait until I hear from Holmes.' The lie came easily and I felt somewhat ashamed at duping my friend, necessary as it was.

Thurston was in too frail a shape to argue or to reason with my statement.

'When you feel able, we'll go downstairs and find you a cab to get you home.'

'That would be very nice,' he said faintly. 'A brandy by my own fireside would be most welcome.'

And so, some ten minutes later I was helping my friend into a hansom after giving instructions to the driver where to take him. Thurston's pale face seemed to glow in the shadows of the cab. 'Sorry about this, Watson. I'm not quite the old campaigner I thought I was.'

'Take care and rest!' I cried, slamming the door and waving to the cabbie to set forth.

As the cab disappeared into the early evening gloom, my weary limbs and aching head indicated that I too was not quite the old campaigner I thought I was.

Fourteen

From Dr Watson's Journal

On reaching Baker Street, the full effect of the blow that I had received, the second in a matter of hours, was having a severe and detrimental effect on me. I staggered up to our sitting room and had just enough energy to slough off my outer coat before slumping down in the armchair by the hearth. I gave silent thanks to Mrs Hudson, who had banked up the fire, and the fingers of flames were just beginning to show through the coals. It would not be long before I had a roaring blaze.

I longed for a restorative brandy, but I just didn't have enough energy to take my tired frame to the drinks table. Instead, I lay back and closed my eyes. I knew that it would not be long before sleep carried me away into restorative oblivion. How long I slumbered I knew not, but I woke with a start, propelled into wakefulness by some horrific dream, the nature of which was lost to me as soon as I opened my eyes. I sat there as the dancing firelight silhouetted on the walls presented a bizarre picture show for me. My neck was stiff and my brain ached and I felt very odd. Suddenly flashes of light began to appear before me, and then faces and images loomed in view briefly before vanishing rather like the flame of an extinguished candle. It was like a wild unnerving tapestry. Indeed, I wondered for a moment if I was really awake. Certainly my mind was playing some kind of game with me. I pulled myself up into a more erect sitting position and stared into the darkness as the images continued. I saw a cottage. Then waves crashing against rocks. There was Holmes on the beach, but the picture was snatched away before I could determine more. Then I saw blood splattered on the sand. A corpse. Dappled sunlight. The dark interior of an inn. Then the pretty face of a girl. She smiled but intangibly her expression changed from one of fear into one of gloating malice, her teeth champing with fury and hate. Then her features seemed to melt like those of a wax dummy placed near heat, eyes widening into dark empty sockets and the mouth slipping open wide into a black silent maw.

The images continued like a mad, fractured lantern show, and all the while my head throbbed and my senses whirled. Gradually, I realised what was happening – I was regaining my memory.

And then the images faded, darkness descended again and I drifted back into deep sleep. I woke some hours later. I felt stiff and cold, the fire having long burned itself out, but strangely I felt relaxed, elated somehow, as though some great burden had been lifted from me. Those blows to my head may have been physically painful but they had, I was sure, been instrumental in restoring to me the lost fragments of my memory. It was as though I had been able to slip the many missing pieces into a large jigsaw puzzle, completing the picture. With more energy than I expected, I rose and acquired that large brandy I had desired many hours before. Its warmth invigorated and enlivened me. I turned up the lamp and returned to my chair once more.

I cast my mind back to that fateful holiday with Holmes. I was determined to track its progress in detail. By doing so, I hoped, indeed

I believed, that it would provide me with the answers to so many of the conundrums which had baffled me in recent days. With great effort, I forced my mind back to recapture those memories. I remembered the train journey down to Totnes, hiring the horse and cart and the drive to the coast. With a thrill, in my mind's eye I saw the cottage on the cliffs, exactly as I had seen it on the day we arrived. I took a large sip of brandy and sat back in the chair, closed my eyes and allowed the whole scenario of what happened next to run through my mind. I was thrilled by the precise details I was now able to recall; the scenes, the conversations, the faces and the names.

Blackwood! That name reverberated in my mind. Of course. Blackwood. Enoch Blackwood, the son of the reviled Bartholomew Blackwood. The young man's face loomed before me, rippling insubstantially. My heart beat faster and my body tensed as the awful realisation washed over me. Yes, I did remember meeting him in Howden and the meal at his strange house, but what made my whole body stiffen with a strange mixture of fear and excitement was the realisation that I had seen the face, the man, since then. I was sure that he was the strange visitor who had come to see Holmes that day I had been sent off to organise tea; the visitor who had disappeared before I returned. He had been here in Baker Street. In these very rooms! Why did I not recognise him, remember him? Why did Holmes not indicate that we had met before? What on earth did it all mean?

I took another gulp of brandy and tried to organise my thoughts, but my brain was in such a whirl, crowded with new puzzles and fresh memories, that I could not think straight. However, one thing was clear to me. I was not meant to know him – not meant to recognise Enoch Blackwood. Somehow, my memory of him had been suppressed. How? Why did I not remember? Had my mind been tampered with? The thought appalled me. And what made this contemplation all the more horrendous was the underlying notion that my friend Sherlock Holmes must have known. Indeed, he must have been complicit in the matter. It seemed that he could not be trusted any more. As I allowed this thought to rise in my mind, I shuddered at the terrible implications it wrought. The whole stability and basis of our relationship was upturned.

It would seem that in some way, the events that took place in Howden had been removed from my memory deliberately so that I could not remember them. Had it been drugs or some cunning form of hypnotism? I forced myself to return to the newly recovered scenes once more, and with as much determination as I could muster I began to run them through my brain again in a cold and dispassionate manner. I wanted to recall as much detail as possible, and in particular I wanted to remember those last moments before darkness fell and I woke up some time later in a hospital bed.

There I was, heading for the little stable in the early morning light. I had just left Holmes in the cottage guarding the corpse that had been such a puzzle and a trial to us. I was eager to prepare the horse and cart for our journey and had no sense of danger or apprehension as I entered the small building. The horse stirred at my approach and pawed the ground with one of its forelegs. I patted his flank and uttered some friendly word of greeting. As I did so, I sensed a movement behind me. Before I had time to turn around, a firm hand had clamped a damp cloth across my mouth, pressing hard with a vice-like grip. A familiar aroma assailed my nostrils. There was no doubt in my mind that the cloth contained a strong dousing of chloroform. The smell was more than familiar to me and in that incomprehensible way one's mind works, even in dramatic situations like this, I was momentarily transported back to the makeshift operating theatres in Afghanistan where chloroform was used liberally on the poor wounded devils to enable us to ease their pain while we attempted to save their lives. It was with thoughts and images of that time that I succumbed to the powerful fumes and sank to the ground unconscious.

The next thing I remember was waking up in some dark and damp environment. It was a lofty chamber with a vaulted ceiling, illuminated by burning torches fastened to the walls. I was seated in a large wooden chair and my feet and hands were tied, thus preventing me from moving. Some distance off there were some shadowy figures, who on seeing me raise my head and rouse myself from my drugged slumbers moved towards me. There were four men, three of whom I recognised. There was the man who claimed to be the Reverend Simon Dickens, Enoch Blackwood and Holmes. The other man kept himself in the shadows and I could see only his silhouette, which seemed wiry and crabbed, his back curved with age.

Holmes gazed at me with a kind of vague curiosity, but gave no sign of concern at my plight or made any attempt to release me. His features lacked any sign of strong emotion at all.

'Let me go at once!' I cried, pulling at my bonds.

'Do not distress yourself, Doctor Watson. We mean you no harm,' said Dickens.

'Then why am I trussed up like this? Holmes, what on earth is going on?'

My friend gazed at me with a strange benevolent smile haunting his lips but he said nothing. I had seen him behave like this before, in the old days when in the thrall of one of his lengthy cocaine sessions, when the power of the drug had overwhelmed his senses and composure. But that was in the old days. He had long given up the habit, accepting at last the damage it threatened to his mental powers. Surely he had not relapsed? No, of course not. Something much stronger than cocaine had taken control of him. Gazing at him in the flickering light, it appeared that all emotion and concern had been drained from him. Here was just the shell of the man. It was clear to me that I was in some kind of danger and yet Holmes did nothing to help me; indeed, it seemed that he was in league with the others.

'Holmes, untie me now,' I urged him, but he gave no reaction to my plea.

'Do not distress yourself, Doctor,' said Dickens. 'All will be well. There is no cause for alarm.'

'If that is the case why am I bound in this fashion?'

'In order that we might administer your medicine. It is imperative that we do so.' It was Enoch Blackwood who uttered this statement and as he moved closer to me I saw that he was holding a cup which contained some greenish liquid.

'Your medicine,' he intoned softly. 'It will make you a lot better.'

'I am not ill. Let me go.'

'Indeed, we will. After you have taken your medicine.'

'You can go to hell,' I cried, tugging once more on my unyielding bonds.

'Obviously, the patient is going to be difficult, Mr Dickens. I think I shall require your help.'

Dickens grunted and stepped forward. 'It would be easier if you took this of your own volition, Doctor,' he said.

Blackwood held the cup to my lips. I turned my head sideways but not before I smelt the sour pungent odour emanating from the cup.

'Mr Dickens, if you please,' said Blackwood, leaning closer.

Suddenly I found Dickens' hands on my face. With savage and brutish movements, he clamped one hand around my nostrils, while the other snapped open my mouth. I tried to resist but without success. I was held firmly with my mouth agape. Leaning over me Blackwood forced the cup up against my teeth and then slowly he began to pour the foul liquid into my mouth. I tried to spit it out, but my jaw was held open so tightly that I could not prevent the liquid slipping down my throat. As the volume increased, I began to choke and my eyes began to water, but Blackwood continued undeterred until the cup was empty. What were the devils trying to do? Drug me? Poison me? Surely there were easier ways of killing me than forcing me to swallow a fetid brew?

Dickens released his hold and stood back. Although I coughed and sputtered, it was too late to regurgitate the liquid. I had swallowed it, and whatever purpose they had in forcing me to consume the foul concoction they had been successful. Sherlock Holmes looked on, unmoved and emotionless, as though he were staring at a stone wall.

Was this a mad dream from which I was about to wake up in my bed in Baker Street? Oh, if only that were the case. I screwed my eyes up momentarily in a desperate and childish attempt to make everything go away.

But it did not.

Everything remained as it was. Except now my vision began to blur and my thoughts began to scramble. For some unaccountable reason I chuckled. What was happening to me? Of course, it was the drink. The potion. The draught. The poison. I chuckled again as I failed to find any more synonyms for the drink that had been forced upon me.

What on earth was happening to me?

I have only been really drunk twice in my life and the feelings I was experiencing now were of a similar nature to those I felt on those two occasions. My limbs seemed to have lost any kind of firmness or strength and my tongue seemed to have swollen to fill my mouth. Conversation was nigh impossible: I could not form any kind of coherent sentence. My head ached and I was losing the ability to think clearly.

From the shadows the old man shambled towards me. He was thin and wizened. His paper-thin skin, like an ancient papyrus, was so taut against his face that he looked like a walking skeleton, with fierce eyes blazing in the hollows of his face. His appearance should have frightened me, but my senses were so far adrift from their normal functioning that I just gazed at him in a dreamy fashion as he reached out with his scrawny hand and placed it upon my forehead. I felt the hard fingers scratching on my flesh like the cold claws of some giant bird. His ancient eyes gazed into mine and he began to speak. The words emerged through the thin slit of his mouth, although his lips did not seem to move. The voice was eerie, like the creaking of some ancient door. What he spoke made no sense to me at all. If it was in some foreign language it was certainly not one I had heard before, but this did not concern me in the least for I already felt my whole being floating away on a raft of blessed sleep. As my eyelids grew heavy, I was aware that I was smiling. The odd words reverberated in my ears as greyness cloaked me, a greyness that darkened into deep black. I was now in some sable void, at peace apart from the strange chanting of the old man, which I still heard in my head.

And then suddenly there was nothing.

I was nowhere.

The world was beyond me.

Fifteen

From Dr Watson's Journal

As I sat in the darkness in our Baker Street sitting room I shuddered at the realisation that this memory had been hidden from me until now. The blows to my head had somehow dislodged it from its hiding place. It had been deliberately suppressed, no doubt by the powers of that strange brew that I had been forced to ingest. However, this unpleasant revelation did nothing to help me pierce the veil of mystery that surrounded me. Desperately, I tried to make some sense of it. If this drug I had taken could trick the memory in such a fashion, then no doubt Enoch Blackwood and Dickens could have held Holmes in their power by similar means. Remembering his blank face in that dank cellar, it was clear that he was under some kind of spell, maybe held in some kind of hypnotic trance. That must be the answer. The powerful, independent strength of my friend's intellect which had proved no match for such mind games in the past had in some way been undermined. By whatever dastardly means at their disposal these villains had managed to coerce him, bend him to their wishes. Certainly in his right mind he would never have allowed them to treat me as they did.

However, what continued to puzzle me was what happened next. After I sank into oblivion, what did they do with Holmes? What did they want from him? And why did they let me live? The next thing I knew, the next thing I actually remembered, was waking up in the hospital bed some weeks later with no memory or knowledge of how I got there. At the time, I vaguely recalled entering the little stable, but did not remember where it was or any of the events that preceded that moment. Gradually, I regained my strength and the ability to eat and converse. I was informed that I was in a private nursing home near Richmond and that I had been there for nearly a month. I was shocked by the news that I had been unconscious for so long, but desperate as I was I could not piece together any of the incidents that had occurred leading up to my blackout. The doctor, a young Scotsman with a deferential air, told me that I had succumbed to a fever that had overcome my central nervous system, which had effectively shut down in order for me to recover naturally, but slowly. 'No doubt,' he averred, 'your condition is the result of some bug or virus you picked up when you were out in Afghanistan and it has been lying dormant all these years.'

His diagnosis seemed strange to me, but then I was still groggy from my prolonged sleep and the drugs that had been administered by the medical staff. My brain was not up to the strain of analytical thinking.

Holmes came to visit me from time to time. I learned that it was through his beneficence that I had been cared for at this private clinic. 'It's the least I could do for my old friend,' he said smiling. 'I'm just glad to see you back in the land of the living.'

He was cheerful and kindly, but vague and circumspect about the period leading up to my collapse. I thought at the time that he did not want to weary me with details but I realised now that it was a definite ploy on his part to keep me from the truth. As I regained strength and confidence, I was eventually allowed to return to London, to Baker

Street, where dear Mrs Hudson made such a fuss of me and took on the role of nurse. Rest interspersed with a series of walks in the various London parks soon had me feeling more like my old self again. However, there was still that gaping hole in my memory that neither time, nor my friend, seemed able to fill.

While I believed that I was returning to normal, Holmes, on the other hand, seemed a somewhat different person. At first I thought that it was my illness and my weakened state that made it seem as though he had altered in some way, but as I regained my health, I began to change my mind. There was nothing terribly obvious in his behaviour that denoted the change. Only someone who knew him as well as I did, knew his humours, foibles and habits as intimately as I did could have appreciated the subtle differences. There was something distant, reserved in his behaviour towards me. On the surface his actions seemed natural enough, but the manner in which they were executed seemed mechanical and routine, lacking the truth of feeling and genuine sentiment. And then there were his eyes; usually so bright and hawk-like in appearance, they now seemed dull and listless like those of a blind man. At first I wondered if he had in fact returned to his old drug-taking habit but there really was no other evidence to suggest this.

Of course, because of my convalescence, I was excluded from accompanying Holmes on his investigative sojourns and it had almost become routine now that he excluded me from his detective work. The cries of 'when you are strong and well enough' had faded and he just carried on silently, almost secretly, as though he was deliberately excluding me from his activities.

I rose from my chair and replenished my glass with another tot of brandy. I made a futile effort to revive the faded fire, but the embers were too weak to be resuscitated. I gave a shrug and took a drink. The brandy will have to warm me in lieu of the flames, I mused with a wry smile. So, I thought, having brought my memories up to date and now more or less complete, I am still faced with a conundrum. I cast my mind back to earlier that day, when in that monstrous disguise Sherlock Holmes had assured me that all his strange behaviour had been in my best interests. What were his words?

'It would be inconvenient for you to remember. You must trust me in this matter, Watson. You must stop your investigations and be satisfied to be kept in the dark for the moment.'

For whatever reason, how could he be so inconsiderate? I had been in the dark for several months now. To remain adrift on this sea of ignorance was untenable. My friend did not seem to care about this. Suddenly I grew angry. I know in the past there had been occasions when Holmes had excluded me from his plans, been secretive and kept vital information from me, but this was always in the pursuit of a successful conclusion to an investigation. His actions had in no way affected my wellbeing or been detrimental to me personally. This was not the case here. My health, my mental stability had been seriously affected by a series of incidents of which he was fully cognisant and I was not. Holmes had deliberately kept me from the truth. Indeed he had admitted that my recollections had been 'wiped'. Wiped! Like a damp cloth rubbed across a blackboard so that all the chalk writing was obliterated. And Sherlock Holmes, my friend, if indeed I could still consider him as such, had colluded in such a procedure.

My anger grew as I turned these thoughts over in my mind. I felt my grip tightening around the brandy glass and my body stiffen as my emotions flamed within me. This charade had to stop. I was no longer prepared to be played with like a puppet and used at others' whims. Holmes might expect me to sit demurely in Baker Street and wait. But wait for what?

In the heat of my anger, with a speed that surprised me, I concocted a plan of action. The clouds parted and I knew what I must do, how I must act to get to the bottom of this grave business. I was determined to expose the mystery at the heart of it and to restore both my sanity and wellbeing once and for all.

The first thing I did was retire to my room for a good night's sleep. Strangely, despite my new resolve and my active mind, very soon after pulling the covers over me, I fell into a deep and untroubled sleep. I awoke around seven and I felt refreshed and eager to implement my plans. I carried out my ablutions with speed and efficiency, dressed and requested a light breakfast of scrambled eggs, toast and coffee from Mrs Hudson.

'Mr Holmes away again,' she said, laying the tray down on the table.

'Yes, for some days I gather.'

'Well, it's good to have you about the place again looking like your old self.'

'It's good to be here,' I smiled, 'but I'm afraid I shall be away for a few days myself. I have some business out of town.'

'Oh, you busy gentlemen. Ah, well, you take care, Doctor Watson,' she said as she made for the door.

'I will,' I replied.

As I ate my breakfast, I ran over the details of what I intended to do. I felt calm and in control and more composed than I had done for many a long day. I had not spent years sharing rooms and adventures with Sherlock Holmes without absorbing some of his skills. Today I was going to prove that I was a very apt pupil indeed. My confidence was so strong that I felt no need to rush into action. I allowed myself the luxury of savouring a post-prandial smoke before I commenced my first task – which was house breaking.

Well, not quite house breaking as such, but gaining entrance to a locked room. The room in question was Sherlock Holmes' bedroom. It was in here that he kept his most private papers. In all the years I'd been domiciled in Baker Street I had rarely been inside the room and on those occasions I could tell by Holmes' quick movements and furtive glances that he was not happy with my presence there. It was as though the room contained some guilty secret that he was afraid I would see. Guilty secret? Well, maybe there was one. Today, I might find out.

The room was locked but it was an old-fashioned mechanism and I had learned the process of picking such pieces from the master. I borrowed Holmes' burgling kit, which he kept in a drawer in our sitting room, and within a few minutes I had released the lock. Turning the handle, I gently pushed the door open.

The room was in darkness. The curtains were pulled across and where they failed to meet exactly in the middle a thin splinter of light pierced the gloom. With a kind of reckless, dramatic gesture I tugged the curtains back, allowing daylight to flood into the room. The furnishings were spartan. There was a desk in the corner, a wash stand, a wardrobe, a small bookcase and a bed, by which stood a table piled with books and papers. I well remembered spending an uncomfortable time hidden behind that bed in the Culverton Smith poisoning case.

Pushing this memory aside, I made a beeline for the bedside table, for surely here was his most recent bedtime reading. On the top of the pile was an ancient tome which had several pieces of paper inserted as bookmarks. The title of the book both chilled and thrilled me. It was *Sansom's History of Witchcraft and Devil Worship.*

I sat on the bed and opened the book. The first section that had been referenced by a bookmark provided a potted biography of Bartholomew Blackwood and told me little that I did not already know, but the second section a few pages later was much more revealing. It related to Blackwood and his evil ambition to bring forth the Devil incarnate into the world by means of a ritual known as 'Corpus Diablo'. It had been Blackwood's greatest ambition and it would seem that he had never managed to bring together all the elements requisite for such an abominable ceremony to take place. The time, the location, the arcane rituals and the vessel – the recipient of the Devil's satanic spirit – all had to be in accord. Apparently, Blackwood had spent his life seeking the essential incantations and ceremonial procedures. They were drawn from the Devil-worshipping sects at various periods in history: from the Egyptians, the Incas, the Salem Brethren and the Hellfire Club. Sansom assured his readers that there was one new and original incantation based on the researches of a certain Italian satanist in the seventeenth century that needed to be added to this blasphemous mixture. Ironically, the location had to be a Christian church and the receptacle – as the author referred to him – was the body of a man ready for the Devil to inhabit. This was not any ordinary man, however. He was to be of refined intellect and 'god-like standing in his community' and, strangely enough, an agnostic. The time was also crucial: midnight on All Hallows' Eve, the 31st of October.

I flicked through the book to see if there were any further reference points left by Holmes or indeed any other sections which related to Blackwood or the ceremony of Corpus Diablo. There did not seem to be, but there was one other feature of the book that secured my attention and sent shivers of fear up my spine. In the closing pages there was a brief biography of the author, Gilbert Sansom. I read with chilling fascination that he had been at one time inhabitant of 'the isolated hamlet of Howden in Devonshire'. Like lightning strikes, images of the cottage, the village and the old church flashed before my eyes. These visions only served to confirm my conviction that the solution and explanation to the mystery that had enveloped me and Sherlock Holmes lay back in Devon in that 'isolated hamlet' of Howden.

Sixteen

From Dr Watson's Journal

I knew that I was being followed before I reached the end of Baker Street. A tall fellow in a grey ulster seemed particularly interested in me as soon as I stepped out onto the pavement. I had first noticed this man when I had peered out of the window to observe the weather. There he was, across the street, apparently reading a sporting newspaper, leaning casually against the wall. I thought nothing of it at the time, but when he was still there nearly an hour later, still perusing the same paper, my suspicions were aroused. Obviously the coven was watching the place. He might, I mused, be one of Holmes' men put there to watch me and make sure I didn't try to interfere with his activities, whatever they may be, or he could be a cohort of another party whose name I could not bear to mention even to myself. Whoever was his master, I had to lose him. I neither needed nor wanted a shadow.

It did not take me long to shake him off. Indeed, it was quite pleasurable to do so. With ease I managed to slip down a few side streets and double back on myself a couple of times. Within ten minutes I had lost my shadow and secured a cab and was on my way to Paddington Station, leaving Mr Grey Ulster behind in the warren of streets to the east of Baker Street somewhere chasing his tail.

I had to wait for over an hour for a train to Totnes but I moved about the station, never staying in one spot more than five minutes while maintaining constant vigilance. I knew that it was not beyond the bounds of possibility that my enemies had lookouts planted at all the major termini in London – and especially this one, which had trains that would carry me to the West Country, down towards Howden.

All seemed well when I boarded the train and I made my way straight to the restaurant car. Not only did this suit me, as I was beginning to feel hungry, but it is a much more public place than a carriage, where one can easily be isolated and accosted. I chose the set lunch and devoured it with relish. Then I sat back to view the passing scene through the window: the tall grimy buildings and tenements of the city were soon left behind, replaced by the neat properties of the suburbs, which in turn gave way to the countryside. The rolling fields and wooded copses were far from lush and verdant as they had been when Holmes and I had first travelled on this route earlier in the summer. Although it was only autumn, there were already signs of winter's breath shrivelling the leaves and fading the green of the grass. I knew that all seasons had their beauty, but in my current mood, the harshness and grimness of winter waiting in the wings seemed depressing and bleak. In many ways, the countryside suited my feelings: it matched my dark forebodings concerning my venture. Although I was being active again and I had a purpose after many weeks of inactivity, I really had no clear scheme in prospect or great hopes concerning the outcome of my actions. I knew I had to visit Howden again and snoop around to see what I could discover but this was hardly a carefully organised investigation. All I could do was be ready to act and react appropriately as events unfolded.

'Excuse me, is this seat taken?' The voice broke into my reverie and I replied automatically with my usual courtesy before my senses had a chance to gauge the wisdom of my response. 'No, it is free,' I said casually.

And then I gazed up at the speaker. He was a tall young man with a handsome face and a pair of piercing blue eyes. He carried a grey ulster over his arm.

'Thank you,' he said with a brief smile, which did not reach his eyes. With sharp deft movements, he pulled the chair away from the table and seated himself opposite me, placing the ulster on his lap.

I had no doubt that my fellow diner was the man who had followed me from Baker Street. Somehow he had picked up the scent and caught up with me. Possibly he had worked out that I would be making for Paddington Station to catch a train to Devonshire. His steely glance and the tight smirk on his lips confirmed that he was not a friend.

'Good to see you again, Doctor Watson. You were in such a hurry this morning,' he observed in a bright theatrical fashion.

'What do you want?' I asked abruptly. I was in no mood for artificial chit-chat.

He raised his eyebrows and pursed his lips. It was a sarcastic response to my query.

I made to rise from my seat but he leaned forward until his face was but a few inches away from mine. 'Stay where you are. For the moment you are going nowhere. I had better warn you that I have a pistol concealed under my coat. I shall not hesitate to use it if you do not… behave yourself.'

I did not doubt his word.

Just at that moment, the waiter came down the aisle carrying a large pot of coffee. On reaching our table and observing that I had finished my meal, he enquired if I required coffee.

'Yes please,' I said, proffering my cup. He leaned forward and poured the steaming brew. As soon as the coffee reached the brim of my cup, I threw the contents into the face of my dining companion, before pulling the tablecloth, sending the crockery in all directions and upending the table. The Grey Ulster man gave a cry of shock as the hot liquid scalded his face. As he fell backwards off his chair, the table and its assorted contents landed on top of him with a jangling crash. The waiter stepped sideways in amazement, dropping the coffee pot at his feet. In the resultant confusion, I made a quick exit from the dining compartment.

I knew that I was reacting to events on an instinctive level without thinking rationally of the consequences. I had escaped from my enemy, but as I raced down the corridor of the next carriage I wondered, with a growing sense of panic, what I was going to do now. My trick with the coffee and the overturned table had allowed me to escape the Grey Ulster man's clutches momentarily, but had only bought me a little time. It would not be long before he was haring after me. What was I to do? Moving down the train as I was, I would eventually reach the last carriage and be an easy target for a fellow with a loaded pistol.

As I reached the next carriage I had decided on a plan of action. Or rather, to be precise, I realised there was only one thing I could do.

I pulled the communication cord.

Within seconds, there was an almighty screech and the train juddered violently as though the whole thing was going to tumble from the rails. I reached the carriage door and gazed out as the rolling fields and straggly hedges slowed down before my eyes. Compartment doors slid open and inquisitive heads appeared.

Cries of 'What's going on?' 'Is there an accident?' 'Why are we stopping?' filled the air.

The train was almost at a halt when I flung open the carriage door and jumped from the train into the long grass at the side. I quickly picked myself up and, keeping a low profile in a hunched posture, I slithered down the slope, clambered over a small fence and ran into a small wood at the bottom. Once there, under the shadows of the canopy of branches, I turned and glanced back. I could just see a section of the train through the trees. Faces crowded at the windows and there was a tremendous hullaballoo and the sound of a whistle. Strangely, despite the desperate situation I was in, I could not help but smile. The sight was reminiscent of a *Punch* cartoon. All it needed was a wittier scribe than I to come up with an amusing caption.

With this thought temporarily lightening my spirits, I turned on my heels and sped deeper into the woods. I was undecided whether to follow the rough path that snaked its way through the trees or make my own way through the undergrowth. I knew if I did the latter, it would be less likely that I would be spotted but at the same time my progress would be slower. However, I reasoned that the path obviously led somewhere, hopefully to some hamlet or farmstead. For that reason I chose the path. I trotted along, constantly casting glances behind me to see if I had been followed. I observed nothing but trees and all I could hear was the hushing rustle of the autumn leaves above my head as they swayed in the breeze.

After I had travelled for about a mile, the path split into two sections. I chose the track that led east, hoping that I was roughly following the line of the railway. I had no idea where I was or how far I was from Totnes, but I assumed that if I followed the path of the railway, I would come upon a station where I would be able to resume my journey. I hoped that this would not be long. My sudden dramatic departure from the train meant that I had left my luggage and overcoat behind and already I was beginning to feel the chill of autumn in my bones.

With my chest heaving from my exertions – I was not used to such exercise after a long time in hospital – I slowed my pace down to a brisk walk. After about half an hour the trees began to thin out and

I saw some distance ahead of me glimpses of a range of undulating fields. Just then I heard a sharp crack as though someone had stepped on a dry branch and had snapped it in two. I turned quickly and gazed behind me. As I did so, I glimpsed a shadow darting between the trees about a hundred yards away. My pulse began to race as I realised that the sound I heard was not a snapping branch but was in fact a gunshot. As if to confirm this realisation, there came another. I felt the bullet whiz close by me. I dropped to the ground and wriggled into the denser undergrowth. Raising my head slightly I peered into the arboreal gloom, in search of the sniper. I saw a quick flash of him as he moved forward with speed in a zigzag fashion, finally coming to rest behind a large oak tree some twenty feet away from me. Although I could not make out any distinctive features – my assailant was a mere shadowy blur – I had no doubt that this was my cursed limpet, Mr Grey Ulster, who had followed me from the train. What made my predicament all the more perilous was the fact that I could not return fire: my own revolver was stowed in the inner pocket of my overcoat which had been left behind on the train.

Raising myself into a crouching position, I picked up a small branch and hurled it to my left, while veering to my right. As the branch landed some distance away, another shot rang out. Keeping low to the ground and moving as silently as I could I retraced my route, so that I was able to circle behind the oak tree where my assailant was hiding. As I did this, he edged forward until he gained the protection of another tree. I could see him clearly now, his pale face taut and exultant in the dim light. He seemed to be enjoying the hunt. Retrieving a small log from a tangle of weeds, I moved closer to him, approaching from behind. As he continued to peer ahead, waiting to catch a glimpse of me, I managed to creep up from the rear. I was almost upon him when he sensed my presence and turned. As he did so I brought the log down upon his head with great force. He had moved too swiftly for it to be an accurate hit and it only caught him a glancing blow on the forehead. However, it had the power to knock him down and as he fell backwards his gun went off, the bullet firing harmlessly into the branches above. I stomped on his wrist with my foot and with a cry of pain he released his weapon, which skittered away into a pile of mouldy leaves. I raised the log to strike him again, but he kicked out violently with his feet, knocking me off balance. I stumbled backwards, only just managing to maintain my equilibrium.

With great alacrity, my opponent jumped to his feet and rushed towards me with a savage cry. However, I was ready for him and I swung the log with great force. This time my aim was very accurate. It smashed hard against his jaw and he fell to the ground with an agonised cry. Under normal circumstances I am not a violent man but in this situation I realised that unless I rendered my assailant unconscious, my life was in peril. With this in mind, I raised the log again with the intention of finishing the job.

With amazing spirit and energy, my enemy rolled away from my range and scrambled to his feet. He gazed at me, eyes ablaze with hatred, his features dripping with blood from the wound on his face and smeared with mud. With a sudden movement, he pulled a knife from the inside of his jacket and, uttering a feral cry which echoed through the wood, he leapt at me. For an instant I froze with shock and indecision but then, just in the nick of time, my self-preservative instincts took over and I swung the log once more. My aim was wild and I missed him completely. Within seconds, he had launched himself on me. The force of his attack knocked us both to the ground where we grappled like fairground wrestlers. I released my hold on the log and grasped the wrist of my assailant which held the knife in an attempt to keep it away from my face. He grunted and groaned as he fought hard against me and I feared that he was winning this particular battle. I pressed hard against him and with a twist of my body we rolled over so that I was on top of him. This weakened his hold and I was able to push his arm away. He flexed his muscles against this move but with my superior position, he failed. He made a dramatic stab at me with the knife. With great force, I deflected the blow, wrenching his arm backwards, the blade sinking into his own breast. He gave a gurgling sigh and his eyes widened with shock and then flickered wildly like the wings of an errant butterfly before closing. Closing forever. Almost immediately a damp crimson patch spread across his chest.

I pulled away, half in horror and half, I must confess, in relief. I stood for some moments staring down at the dead man and in particular at the growing red stain as the blood oozed from the wound. It wasn't the first time I had been responsible for a man's death, but never in such dramatic circumstances. It was not an outcome that I had desired. It was purely the result of an action of self-defence but that did not stop me from feeling guilty and somewhat depressed.

Of course the question that thundered in my brain was 'Why?' Why had this man been so determined to kill me – or at least prevent me from visiting Howden? What terrible intrigue had enmeshed me? And enmeshed I was. There certainly was no escape from this dangerous tangled skein. And there was no going back. I was reminded of the words of Macbeth: 'It was as tedious to turn back as go o'er.'

I felt in my pocket and retrieved my cigarette case and, incongruous as it was, I sat on a fallen log and had a smoke. It helped to ease my jagged nerves and enabled me to bring my situation into focus. I knew that I had to press ahead and find my way to Totnes. After extinguishing my cigarette, I examined the dead man's clothing to see if I could find any information or clues to help bring some light to the mystery. However, all I discovered was a wallet with some cash, a pocket watch, handkerchief and a packet of headache powders. Nothing of consequence.

I relieved the fellow of his ulster. That at least would help protect me from the growing cold. Then I covered the body with some dead leaves and continued on my way.

Seventeen

Created from Notes made by Sherlock Holmes

Enoch Blackwood came into the room, his brow puckered with concern. 'I have news that Watson has left Baker Street,' he said simply. 'It is most likely that he will be heading for Howden.'

Sherlock Holmes, who was seated by the fire, glanced up at Blackwood, his eyes registering no emotion.

'So,' continued Blackwood, 'despite all your efforts and our allowances, it looks as if there is no hope for your friend. He seems determined to bring about his own destruction. It is a shame, but this turn of events does not alter things from your point of view. I hope you realise that.'

Holmes did not reply, but returned his glance to the flickering flames.

Part Three

Eighteen

From Dr Watson's Journal

Dusk was falling rapidly by the time I reached the road. After trudging for ages across sodden fields, at last I found myself on a manmade pathway. My problem now was to gauge which way to travel. I assumed that I turned to the west, but it was a guess only. Trying hard to dismiss the faint clouds of despair which began to form in my mind, I set forth with a will. As good luck would have it, after about twenty minutes of tramping, I heard the sound of horses' hooves and the rattle of a carriage behind me. On turning, I saw a farm cart trundling down the road in my direction. I waved and called to the driver, a shadowy figure in rough workman's clothing. He brought the vehicle to a halt some yards away from me.

'By heaven, you gave us a fright, loomin' out o' the darkness like that,' he said with some passion.

I apologised and asked if he could give me a ride to the nearest town or village. He treated my request with some reluctance. 'Where you be headed?'

'Well, I want to get to Totnes.'

He whistled and pushing his cloth cap back he scratched his head. 'Why, that be miles away, sir.' He thought for a moment, his craggy face twitching as his mind paraded through a range of mixed thoughts. 'Tell you what, sir, I'm headed back to the farm now. I could give you a bed for the night and drive you to Tansy Halt station tomorrow morning. You should be able to catch a train to Totnes from there.'

'That is wonderful,' I said, my tired face breaking into a smile. 'So very kind. I will pay for your hospitality, of course.'

'As you see fit, sir, but there bain't no need. It's a poor old world if a fellow can't do a favour for another fellow who's got a problem. And you got a problem, bain't you, sir?'

'You've gone a long way to solve it,' I said, my grin broadening.

He matched my smile, his lips parting to expose a row of uneven yellow teeth. He extended his hand to me. 'Pull yourself up on the wagon, sir, and we'll be off.'

I did as I was bidden, and before long we were rattling down the lane towards a distant farmstead whose lights twinkled in the darkness.

My host was Jacob Weatherall, and his wife, who was as obliging and gracious as her husband, made me feel very welcome and provided me with hot food and a warm bed for the night. Neither asked me how I had landed up in a lonely spot in Devon without luggage or why I needed to get to Totnes. They were a simple couple and said little, but their Christian goodness was wonderfully reassuring and I felt humbled in their company.

As I made my way up to my sleeping quarters, Jacob touched me on the arm. 'I reckon you are right keen to get to Totnes, sir, so I'll get you up 'fore cock crow so's we can be on the road before it gets light. Then you can catch an early train at Tansy Halt.'

I nodded. 'Thank you.'

And so it was that by nine o'clock the following morning I was boarding a little stopping train at Tansy Halt and waving goodbye to Jacob Weatherall. He had refused any financial compensation for his kindness and hospitality, but I managed to slip several sovereigns into his ragged jacket pocket without his knowledge. I had been informed that the journey would take about ninety minutes, so once more I was on course.

I saw him as soon as I stepped out of the station at Totnes. A stocky fellow in a shabby overcoat with a walrus moustache dominating his piggy features. On catching sight of me as I emerged into the sharp autumn sunlight, he seemed to jump to attention. Positioned by the tea stall, he did look a little out of the ordinary, contrasting with the throng of other passengers. But what also drew my attention to him was the fact that I remembered his face. I had seen it before. I recalled exactly when I had seen it before. He had been one of the men lounging outside The Dark Man in Howden, the day Holmes and I had met Enoch Blackwood. He had cheered on one of the fighters who had been involved in the impromptu brawl. The one with the missing buckle from his shoe. In other words: he was another of them, the devils who were determined that I should not reach Howden. He had no doubt been placed on sentry duty to keep an eye out for me in case I managed to give Mr Grey Ulster the slip.

I was undecided what to do in this situation. I was very tempted to step up to the blackguard and challenge him, but no doubt he would be armed and I decided that this was not a wise move. It was too early in the day, I mused, for a gunfight in a public place. I had to be more cunning than that.

My original intention on reaching Totnes was to visit the farrier who had supplied Holmes and me with a horse and trap when we came down in the summer and to arrange for the hire of a similar conveyance to take me to Howden. Now I realised that before I could make this arrangement, I had to deal with my moustachioed friend in some way first.

Strangely, this thought actually amused me. Glancing over at his porcine features I reckoned that my shadow was not a fellow of the greatest intellectual prowess. Brute force maybe, but brains, no. The eyes, small and dim, did not radiate any sense of cunning or intelligence. I reckoned that it should not tax my ingenuity too much to get the better of this fellow.

Whether it was because I'd had no breakfast and was a little light-headed or that the events of the last few days had made me more reckless than usual, I do not know, but I felt like playing with this particular pawn in the dark game in which I was now involved. I wandered around the streets of Totnes aimlessly, sometimes slowing down to an almost lethargic pace and then suddenly speeding up for no reason at all. I doubled back on myself several times, but I always made sure that I was in full view of other people. I knew it would be dangerous to move into a side street where he and I would be alone.

Finally, I stepped inside a tea room. My shadow remained outside. After ordering tea and crumpets, I left my seat and passed through a door which I assumed led through into the kitchen.

'I'm afraid customers are not allowed in here,' said a pert young girl, busy preparing some sandwiches.

'I'm here to see Mrs Laidlaw,' I said, with some gravitas. I had noted her name as the proprietress over the door as I entered.

'She is in the office but…' the girl tried to inform me, but I brushed past her to the end of the kitchen where I had spotted an outer door.

'Sir…!' the girl cried, but I had already opened the door and was out into a lane at the rear of the premises before she could say more.

I found myself chuckling as I sped down the lane, strangely amused at my subterfuge. It made me smile to think of my piggy-faced friend waiting patiently for me outside the front of the premises. As I passed on to one of the main streets, I checked that the villain was nowhere in sight and then by a circuitous route, I made my way to the farrier's to hire a pony and trap. On the way there I called in at a grocer's to buy a few provisions.

Within half an hour I was trotting along narrow country roads towards my destination. The lightness of my mood had evaporated as I now realised that I was approaching the most difficult and perilous part of my mission – a mission that was, I had to admit, rather vague. I was not sure exactly what I was going to do once I had reached the village. Going to Howden, visiting the inn and the home of the Blackwoods in search of Holmes could well be the most foolhardy and dangerous thing I could do. Perhaps it would be as well to wait until nightfall when at least the cover of darkness would give me some protection. I was sure the answer to the conundrum lay in the village but the problem was how I was going to unlock it.

I decided that the best thing would be to make my way to Samphire Cottage first of all and see if I could make it my base. It would be unlikely to be occupied so late in the season. With this simple plan in mind, I urged the pony onwards. As I travelled, the weather changed as though to suit my mood and apprehensions. The bright sunlight of the morning had faded, to be replaced by grey scudding clouds and a cool autumn wind, which penetrated the folds of my coat.

It had begun to drizzle by the time the sea came into view, the darkening sky reaching down to its rippling sable breakers to create a uniform dun-coloured vista.

The cottage stood as I remembered it, crouching on the cliff top, a splash of white against the grey background. I tethered the horse some distance away and approached it on foot. I was pleased to see that there was no spiral of smoke emerging from the chimney and no lights at the windows.

Moving stealthily I crept forward and peered through the windows of the tiny sitting room. All looked deserted. There was no sign of habitation. I tried the door: it was locked but offered no strong resistance to my shoulder. As I applied my weight to it with some force, it sprang open. Within seconds I was inside.

As I stood in the sitting room, gazing around me, strong memories invaded my consciousness. There were still the strange symbols chalked on the door which seemed, suddenly, to dance before my eyes, and then I saw Holmes curled up in the armchair, a pipe clamped in his teeth as he studied some large tome. I remembered the fire crackling in the grate throwing strange shadows up the rough whitewashed walls. The last time I'd seen this room there had been a corpse...

I shut my eyes tightly and shook my head to dislodge these disturbing images. I must not let visions of the past interfere with my task. That way madness lay. I went into the kitchen and unpacked my small parcel of provisions, and with a mug of water I devoured a slice of cheese, an apple and a chunk of bread. The vittles not only revived my energy but in some strange way also my spirits. As I ate, I stared out of the tiny kitchen window. It had stopped raining now and the clouds lifted to provide an eerie brightness, a final rally of daylight before dusk invaded the sky. The tide was on the turn, racing away from the land in a fusillade of angry rollers. Then I saw it. Down on the beach. Almost like a mirage, as if out of nowhere it came: a shimmering shape wandering slowly across the landscape, mirrored in the wet sheen of the sand. My heart skipped a beat as I realised that it was a human figure: small and slim, vulnerable against the backdrop of bay and sea. I watched, mesmerised, as it made its way in an erratic fashion along the beach and then it began to falter. For a brief moment it became static before crumpling down as in a faint onto the sand.

I raced from the house and made my way down the sandy path to the beach. The figure was still there, a slender silhouette on the shiny wet sand. As I approached, I could see that it was in fact a woman. I knelt down and felt her pulse. It was weak but regular. I brushed back the wet tangled hair from her face. I felt a sharp constriction of the heart as I recognised this creature. It was Arabella Blackwood.

Nineteen

From Dr Watson's Journal

A s I scooped up the young woman in my arms, her eyes flickered open and she gazed up at me in a feverish fashion, not quite focusing on my face.

'I have escaped,' she said dreamily. 'I have escaped.' Her lips formed into a faint smile and then she closed her eyes again. I carried her back to the cottage. She was hardly a burden; her body was so thin and emaciated. Once inside, I laid her on the sofa, and retrieving some blankets from the bedroom, I wrapped them round her. With some reluctance I lit a fire, risking the telltale smoke from the chimney announcing a presence in the cottage. I had to try and get the girl warm. Gradually, she seemed to rouse herself, her eyes opening once more. I helped her to sit up. I had discovered a bottle of brandy in the kitchen cupboard and I poured a small measure into a cup and helped her sip it. She spluttered at first when the liquid hit the back of her throat but eventually the alcohol began to revive her. 'Thank you,' she said softly, turning to face me, and then her eyes widened in surprise. 'It's Doctor Watson, isn't it? John Watson, Sherlock Holmes' friend.'

'Yes, yes it is,' I said with a smile.

'You're alive. Still alive.'

'Of course, my dear. Why shouldn't I be?'

Her face clouded again and tears sprang to her eyes.

'What is the matter, my dear? What has happened to you?'

She shook her head in vague denial, not saying a word.

'When I found you, you said that you'd escaped. Escaped from where?'

'From them. From them.'

'Who?'

'My father and my brother.'

'What!' I cried, baffled by her response.

'They have been keeping me prisoner... for fear I would tell.'

I shook my head in total bafflement. Was the girl in her right mind? Delusional? What on earth did she mean?

'Your father is dead, my dear. And your brother loves you.'

She chuckled mirthlessly. 'You are wrong on both counts.'

'But, Arabella, your father, Bartholomew Blackwood, passed away many years ago.'

'No, no. That is what he wants the world to think. That he came back to England to die. But it isn't true. He returned to carry out his grand plan. He let it be known that he had died of illness and old age. It suited his purpose. There would be no more persecution, no so-called Christian vigilantes seeking to destroy him. If people thought that he was dead he knew that he could carry out his work in peace, unmolested.'

'His work?'

'His life's work: the ceremony of Corpus Diablo. The manifestation of the Devil.'

'My God!'

'*His* God. My father worked, researched and studied for years to bring this to fruition. So many conditions have to be right. When he started Enoch and I were innocent children, not really aware of the true nature of his goal. When we *did* become aware, initially we both rebelled but gradually Enoch succumbed to the ministering of our father. He seduced my brother into satanism. As a mere girl, I did not count enough for my father to exert his efforts with me. I was left alone and I… I suppose I turned a blind eye to their pursuit. There was little else I could do. They were my family. I had no friends to whom I could turn. Without my father and Enoch, I was alone in the world. I've never been strong…'

She shook her head and emitted a strangled sob. 'They gave me food, shelter… and love. Love, after a fashion. Their inverted version of love. They cared for me because I was of their kin but at the same time I was virtually a prisoner. God forgive me for being so weak and tolerant and never trying to leave. However, as the time for the ceremony grew nearer and they involved your friend Holmes I knew the moment was approaching when I must summon enough courage to leave. I must escape.'

My body ran cold as one phrase echoed like the toll of a giant bell in my brain: 'and they involved your friend Holmes'. How on earth did they do this? What foul coercion had they imposed on him? What was Holmes' role in this obscene business? Surely, he would not have aided them voluntarily? I was desperate to question the girl on this matter but my common sense ruled the day and I allowed her to tell me her tale in her own fashion.

'With the help of his French disciples, my father was smuggled back into this country and the rumour was spread that he died shortly afterwards. Enoch had already purchased properties in Howden in readiness. The hamlet was dying. The small population was aged with most of the young folk having gravitated to the towns and so many of the houses were deserted. Within a year we had replaced most of the villagers with my father's followers. Strangely his health revived and he seemed to grow in strength and energy. He continued his work in preparation for the ceremony, helped by Enoch, who was becoming more and more obsessed with the desire – the need – to help fulfil my father's great dream. It may have been wrong of me, but I prayed for my father's death. I thought of escaping, alerting the authorities to what was going on…'

'And why didn't you?' I asked, blurting out the question against my better judgement. I had not wanted to stop the flow of her narrative but my innate frustration got the better of me. Why, I wondered, did Arabella Blackwood stand by while her father and brother planned the most obscene and evil ceremony ever conceived?

I got my answer.

'I was watched twenty-four hours a day. I was in essence a captive of my own family. I was not ill-treated or locked away but I knew that I could not leave. I fear that the fervour was so strong with my father and Enoch that they would have gladly seen me dead rather than have their foul secret exposed.'

I shook my head in disbelief. The horror of the poor girl's situation struck me dumb. Were there such monsters in the world? As soon as this question raised itself in my mind, I felt foolish. The answer was obvious. Of course there were. And in some way Sherlock Holmes was involved with them.

'I was reduced to the role of silent watcher,' Arabella continued. 'I saw everything, knew everything that was being planned but I was helpless to do anything about it. Finally a date was set for the ceremony. The stars and astrological conditions indicated that All Hallows' Eve, that is October 31st of this year, was the ideal date. 1899. We are on the brink of a new century. The old one is dying, the old world is dying. Time for a new beginning. The beginning of the rule of Beelzebub.'

'Good grief,' I spluttered. 'This is appalling.'

Arabella nodded grimly. 'One problem remained, however. They needed a human vessel, a shell to accommodate his Dark Magnificence. My father is too old and frail to stand up to the rigours of such an experience and besides, his satanic history is against him. Enoch, too, is not pure enough. The candidate must be an agnostic, you see. A non-believer. And have a brilliant brain. The candidate they chose…'

'…was Sherlock Holmes.'

'Yes.'

At this terrible revelation a number of pieces in this horrific puzzle suddenly fell into place with chilling, heart-stopping clarity. 'So Holmes was lured down to this village to somehow enmesh him in their foul scheme. Cawthorne at my club was part of the conspiracy…'

'They were all part of the conspiracy. They needed first of all to engage his interest and then through a series of ploys and devices to secure his allegiance.'

'But how on earth could they do that? Holmes may be an agnostic but he is the most moral man I know. Nothing on earth would make him agree to fall in with your father's plans.'

'But he did.'

I faltered. In my heart, I knew she was right. My friend's strange and secretive behaviour all pointed to this appalling truth.

'But how?'

'Through drugs and hypnotism, magic, and also by threats.'

'Threats? I know Sherlock Holmes. He does not fear death. He would rather die than aid and abet these demons.'

'It was not his life that was at risk.'

'I don't understand. If not his life… whose?'

Her eyes widened as she stared directly into my face. 'Yours, Doctor Watson.'

'My… life.'

'They said that if Holmes did not agree to their demands, you would be killed.'

I froze in horror at this statement as a wild turmoil of emotions seemed to overtake me momentarily. If what the girl had told me was true – and I was certain it was – then Holmes' apparently cold and curious attitude towards me had been a calculated ploy to keep me in the dark in order to protect me. My friend had been sacrificing so much to save my life. I was overwhelmed by the notion of this selfless act and for some moments I was unable to speak. I had no idea that Holmes cared so much for me or that he would be prepared to act in this way to keep me out of danger, despite the perilous consequences. Surely, he has some plan in mind, I thought. Surely, by some cunning, devious ploy he means to trick these devils. Surely… But in a strange whirlwind of flashbacks I remembered his odd behaviour over the last few months, including the strange midnight conversation with the skeletal stranger in our Baker Street rooms. It had appeared so amicable, so rational and so secretive. It struck me now that this dark stranger must have been Bartholomew Blackwood.

'Is… is he completely under their power?' I asked at length, as I struggled to come to terms with the situation.

She nodded. 'I am afraid so. They feed him drugs, perform spells and through hypnotism my father is able to control him from a great distance. The power of his mind, refined and strengthened through years of practice and study, is omnipotent. While Holmes may appear normal and awake, it is as though he is kept on a long leash like a dog who is at the beck and call of his master.'

I cursed and ran my fingers through my hair in desperation. 'What can we do? We must stop this madness and save my friend.'

'Stop this madness.' The girl repeated my phrase as though it were a chant. She turned her haunted face towards me and gripped my arm. 'There is only one way to stop this madness now,' she said solemnly, 'and that is to kill Sherlock Holmes.'

Twenty

From Dr Watson's Journal

As Arabella Blackwood spoke these words, the firelight tigering her features with shifting shadows, I felt as though I was in the middle of a nightmare, a night-time concoction of mad scenarios and wild imaginings. Reality was but a moment away, when I would wake and shake off these dreadful concepts and all would be well with the world. This foolish notion lasted but an instant. My senses quickly confirmed that I was awake and I was living the terrible truth.

I knew that by some miraculous means I had to shrug off this cloak of despair which was weighing down on my soul and all but suffocating me. Then a thought struck me.

'Surely, if your father died that would bring this business to a close? He is the key and without the key...'

Surprisingly, she shook her head. 'It has gone beyond that now. Once things were set in place for the ceremony, my father passed on the secrets of the infernal rites to several others, including Enoch. It was important this was done as fears for my father's mortality have grown in recent weeks. Preparations are so far advanced now that any one of five or six individuals could carry out the Corpus Diablo ceremony. The only vulnerable link in the chain is Holmes. Vulnerable in the sense that he is the only one who has been coerced into taking part.'

'Where is he now?'

'There is no hope, Doctor. Do not think about it. If you value your life…'

'Value my life! That is the last of my concerns at the moment. Whatever happens I must stop this ceremony taking place and in the process save the life of my friend.' I grabbed her by the shoulders. 'Where is Holmes now?'

Her eyes opened wide with shock at my violent outburst. 'He is at the house. But if you go anywhere near there they will kill you.'

'They will *try* to kill me. That is a different matter.'

Without another word, I grabbed my coat and raced from the house into the dark night.

I travelled to Howden by cart. There was a full moon sailing in a cloudless blue sky and the rough track to the village was illuminated in a pale blue light. As I drove along, I ran through the new information given to me by Arabella Blackwood, information that had placed a completely new complexion on my life, Sherlock Holmes and the events of the last few months. It all seemed so unreal and yet I knew the situation as I now perceived it was the truth. It must be that Holmes had underestimated the malevolent force of Blackwood and his satanic cronies and he was now completely in their power – as he had been from the time when he entered the church in the village on that fateful night in July.

As the hamlet of Howden came into view, the small higgledy-piggledy arrangement of houses and the church spire black against the evening sky, I pulled the cart off the road and behind a small copse. I tethered the horse and then set off across the fields. I thought it would be much safer to approach the village in this fashion rather than by the main access. I knew that outsiders were not welcome here and in my case, I was aware that my life would immediately be forfeit if I were seen and recognised.

Relying on my sense of direction and what memory I could dredge up from my previous visit, I traversed several fields and crossed a small beck before I reached the back wall of the churchyard. I clambered over the wall and crouching down I waited a while, catching my breath. It was a strange sensation to be back in this overgrown plot which was the location of my last memory of this godforsaken hamlet.

All was quiet apart from the rustling of some nocturnal animals. The church was in darkness and what I could see of the main street beyond also appeared similarly dark and quiet. Keeping low and with as much stealth as I could manage, I made my way through the overgrown wilderness of the graveyard to the lychgate and peered down the main street. There was one single light outside the inn, whose windows were the only ones to radiate any illumination.

With bated breath, I slipped through the gate, and keeping close to the wall, I moved down the street. As I reached the spot across the road from the front of the inn, the door suddenly opened, sending a shaft of light into the street, and a man stepped out onto the pavement. I shrank back into the shadows.

He was a broad-shouldered fellow, quite smartly dressed with a neat beard adorning a large open face. He stood for a moment staring up at the stars, and then took a few steps forward and retrieved a small silver case from his pocket and extracted a cigarette. He lit it with a match which he then threw nonchalantly into the air. With casual amusement he watched its trajectory. As it reached its zenith the light died and the match fell to earth in the middle of the road some ten feet or so away from where I was standing. For a moment the man stared intently at the shadows and it didn't take me long to realise that he had seen me.

Casting his cigarette away, he strode swiftly towards me, a grim expression clouding his features.

'Who the hell are you?' he bellowed.

I knew that any attempt to explain my presence was pointless. As a member of this village, this man was my enemy. I knew I had to take the initiative in this matter. I moved forward to meet him and before he could utter another word I brought my fist hard against his chin.

He gave a brusque gasp and fell backwards, and then remarkably like a rubber ball he bounced back up on his feet. Before I knew it, his hands were around my throat. His face came close to mine and in the dim light I could see his eyes wide with fury and ferocity. I swung my arms wildly, battering him on either side of his head, but his grip did not lessen. I began to splutter and feel weak. With one last effort I stamped my heel down hard on his shoes with all my might. He gave a cry of pain and his fingers slackened around my neck. This was sufficient opportunity for me to thrust the man away and deliver several blows to his face. He was only momentarily distracted and rushed at me again. We tussled, crashing down into the dirt, rolling over and over like children playing some kind of rough game.

As he rolled on top of me, he jerked himself upright, pinning me to the ground. He grinned madly before aiming a blow at my face. I turned my head sideways, pulling away from his oncoming fist. He struck my ear. In turning, I spied a small rock to my right. I stretched my arm as far as I could and made a grab for it. My opponent saw what was afoot and reached for the rock himself. Our fingers met, but mine gained the firmer grasp, and I snatched the stone away and in an instant brought it down on the top of the brute's skull. His eyelids fluttered and his weight shifted sideways. I repeated the blow twice more. With a slow groan, he slid unconscious onto the ground by my side. I lay for some seconds breathing heavily and staring blankly at the night sky as I tried to bring my heart rate down to something approximating normal and my senses under control. Slowly I got to my feet and gazed down on the fellow who had attacked me. A nasty wound glistened at his forehead and rivulets of blood spidered down his face. However, the gentle rise and fall of his chest told me that he was still alive.

I gazed around me. The street was silent and deserted. It seemed that our fight had not attracted anyone's attention. I dragged the unconscious man back towards the wall, into the shadows, and then once again tried to steady my nerves. I knew that I could not wait around for long. Any time now someone else could emerge from the inn and I was fairly certain I was not up to battling another contender.

With some difficulty I raised my unconscious opponent into an upright position and then I hauled him over my shoulder in a fireman's lift. I knew he was a big man, but he seemed to weigh far more than his sturdy frame indicated. I carried him back along the street towards the lychgate, praying that no one would suddenly appear out of the darkness and challenge me.

Once in the graveyard, I dumped the fellow down unceremoniously in the farthest corner between two crooked gravestones, tied my scarf around his mouth and covered him over with dead grass. It would be some hours before consciousness returned to his sore head. I searched his clothing and discovered a small pistol secreted in an inner pocket. I checked it carefully. It was loaded. I realised how lucky I had been that the brute had not managed to retrieve it during our altercation. Realising that this unexpected find could be most useful to me now, I slipped it into my pocket.

I made my way down the street once more with as much speed as I could safely muster. Passing the inn, I took the route out of the village which led to Blackwood's house. Here the path was narrower and darker, the moon only glimpsed occasionally through the branches as they shifted gently in the night air.

As the lane narrowed and the foliage on either side of me grew thicker, I began to feel more uneasy and somehow strangely vulnerable – but to what I could not say. It was as though I were entering a totally alien environment. Alien and inhospitable. I felt as though I was being observed but there was no physical evidence for such feelings. I shook my head in dismay and uttered a sharp sigh of self-reproof. I was letting my imagination get the better of me.

At last I reached the entrance to the driveway of the Blackwood residence. For a few seconds my mind wandered back to the first time I had been here on that bright summer's day and the strange sensations I had felt then. I hesitated for a moment, before passing by the gateposts and moving down the driveway. My hand wandered towards the pistol in my pocket for reassurance. I knew that I was risking not just my life but my very soul to proceed with this venture. I have never thought of myself as brave or singularly courageous, but I believed that when forced into a corner, as I felt I was now, I was equal to the occasion. As I gazed through the bushes at the dark imposing silhouette of the Blackwood mansion, I prayed to God that I was equal to *this* particular occasion.

Twenty-One

From Dr Watson's Journal

I tried to remember the layout of the house. I forced my mind back to my previous visit, picturing the rooms and the geography of the building. The place seemed to be all in darkness as though it was deserted, but that may well be because heavy curtains were hiding any interior lights. I stole around to the side of the house to where the dining room was located and crept up to the window, pressing my ear against the pane. At first no sound was evident and then I heard some movement – maybe the scraping of a chair or the closing of a cupboard. I waited, and after a short interval my patience was rewarded by the muffled murmur of a voice. I could not determine the words, nor identify the speaker apart from it being a man, but at least I knew now that the house was inhabited.

What was I to do? Burst in brandishing my revolver like a desperado from the penny dreadfuls? With chagrin I realised that I really had no plan, just intent. I cudgelled my brain into positive creative thinking. The real purpose of my mission, I told myself, was to rescue Sherlock Holmes. To snatch him away from the brood of Devil worshippers.

I was prepared for him to be reluctant to go, even for him to offer resistance to such action, but it was imperative that I pluck him from the clutches of these villains. It was most likely that he was somewhere in this house, whether as a willing guest or a prisoner. It was my task to find him.

With this in mind, I moved to the back of the building in search of some means of gaining entry without alerting the inmates. It was here that I discovered a flight of steps leading down to what I presumed was a cellar. Carefully I negotiated the crumbling steps and encountered a stout wooden door faintly visible in the shaded moonlight. I tried the large ring handle and to my amazement, the door swung open with ease. I gazed over the threshold at the dark void beyond. With some trepidation, I stepped forward; as I did so the dingy corridor in which I found myself shimmered into pale illumination.

'Ah, Doctor Watson, we have been expecting you.'

The voice came from a tall figure I observed in the shadows. He stepped forward into the light. It was Enoch Blackwood. 'It is so good of you to join us at this very auspicious time.' His voice was polite and urbane but I could not fail to detect the undertone of menace in his delivery.

Suddenly I felt very weak, my arms feeble and unable to move. Blackwood's features seemed suddenly indistinct, as though viewed through a fine mist.

'Do not trouble yourself, Doctor. Just relax and do as I say and all will be well. Come, follow me. The others will be anxious to greet you.' He stretched out his arm in a beckoning gesture and then turned and began to walk towards the far end of the corridor.

Like some automaton, with no will of my own, I followed him, my arms now limply dangling by my sides.

He opened the door at the end of the corridor and led me into a large vaulted chamber set out rather like a meeting hall with chairs. At the far end was a dais which I realised was some kind of altar. There were about a dozen people seated in the room, all of whom turned silently at our entrance, their eyes, emotionless and cold, boring into me.

Blackwood moved down the central aisle between the chairs and like a child, I followed suit. I seemed to have no choice in the matter. I was a puppet to his strange mastery.

The eyes of this strange congregation followed me as I made my way to the dais. It was then that I saw a face I recognised on the front row. It beamed in pleasure at me. That smile drove an icicle through my heart.

The grinning creature was Arabella Blackwood. She blew me a kiss and giggled, her eyes bright with malevolent merriment.

I shuddered with the horror of it all. I had been duped. It had all been a performance on her part to lure me here. Her tale regarding the imprisonment by her father and brother and her desire to escape from the clutches of the satanists had all been a pack of devilish lies. And I had swallowed it whole. By a series of diabolical misdirections and sleights of hand they had played with me, leading me to exactly where they wanted me to be. As a result, I had been trapped. I was in the clutches and at the mercy of this foul brood. At that moment, as my heart constricted with fear and despair, I believed all hope was lost.

But the worst was yet to come.

The figure of a man emerged from behind the screen at the rear of the dais. He was tall, imperious and dressed in a coarse black gown, tied at the waist by a rough cord. He smiled at me and nodded his head in greeting.

It was Sherlock Holmes.

Part Four

From Sherlock Holmes's Journal

I believe that it is important that I note down in detail all the events concerning the Blackwood affair, for it may be the only true record of the matter once the dust has settled. I am aware that it may well bring about my final bow, and if this is to be the case I wish my own record of what occurred to be extant and available for scrutiny in order to dismiss any ill rumours concerning my involvement and to expunge any blame that may fall upon my good friend Watson.

My first intimation of the matter came when I visited my brother Mycroft in his chambers in Pall Mall. He was recovering from a stroke and was facing his incapacity with the fortitude and stoicism which were an innate part of his strong character. He had lost the use of his right arm and his legs were weak, so he was resigned to a wheelchair – 'for the moment, Sherlock, just for the moment.' His brain was as sharp and as active as ever and with the help of his secretary, Chivers, he was able to carry out some of his government duties as normal.

On the afternoon in question, Chivers had served us sherry and biscuits and then had been dismissed by Mycroft so that he could have 'a private discussion with my brother.' That phrase and his hooded eyes told me that this 'discussion' meant business: detective business.

On being left alone, I rose and stared down into the famous thoroughfare below. 'Isn't it a little too soon for you to be involved in cloak and dagger machinations? Surely all your efforts should be concentrated on recovering your health,' I said casually.

'Work is my restorative, Sherlock. I am an automaton. I cannot function without work. You know the syndrome as well as I! And besides, the matter I am about to discuss with you is most urgent and will not wait until I am racing up the steps of the Diogenes Club.'

I laughed out loud. The image was too comic not to. Mycroft had hardly run in his life and the thought of his large bulk bounding up the staircase of his beloved club was wonderfully amusing.

I returned to my seat beside him and leaned forward in readiness to hear what he had to say.

'Have you heard of Bartholomew Blackwood?'

'The satanist?'

Mycroft nodded. 'Well, he certainly worships the Devil.'

'Present tense. I believed he was dead. Perished somewhere in France.'

'That is what he wished the world to believe but I can assure you, brother mine, that the fellow is very much alive and planning the greatest of blasphemies.'

I sipped my sherry and waited for Mycroft to continue.

'Blackwood now lives in Howden, a hamlet in Devonshire, with his son and daughter and has surrounded himself with his wayward followers. They control the village. It is now a satanic community.' He paused and flashed a brief sardonic smile. 'Melodramatic words, I know, but I am afraid they are quite fitting for such a scenario, one which could easily have been ripped from the pages of some gothic romance. Blackwood, the man himself, lives as a hermit in isolation and is rarely seen, even by his followers, but his son and daughter carry out his commands and evil work. They are planning something quite terrible.'

I raised an inquisitive eyebrow.

'It has long been Blackwood's desire – obsession if you like – to carry out a ceremony in which the Devil is conjured in such a form that he inherits the body of a man. The epitome of evil made flesh on earth.'

I laughed. 'This is preposterous,' I said. 'The stuff of dark fairy tales; the work of Stoker or Le Fanu.'

'I have been convinced otherwise. Trust me, Sherlock. You know full well that I bear the same fierce shaft of rationality and common sense in my soul as you but at the same time, I have an open mind. I have consulted experts in demonology and the occult and despite my sturdy scepticism, I have been convinced that such an event, a procedure is... not impossible.'

I could see from my brother's sturdy gaze and furrowed brow that he spoke with great conviction. I knew from past experience that when Mycroft expressed an opinion as fact he was always correct. But how could I, a man who worships at the altar of rationality, accept this wild and whirling concept?

It was now Mycroft's turn to smile at me. 'I know exactly what you are thinking, but in this matter I must ask you to trust me. To trust me implicitly. Because, you see, you are directly involved.'

At these words my response faltered on my tongue.

'Let me explain. One of the experts in the occult I consulted, Professor Julius Krasinski of Prague University, told me that for this particular ritual – Corpus Diablo – to be carried out successfully, so many circumstances must be in place. For instance, it is essential that the ceremony is performed on one of the main sabbats of the year – All Hallows' Eve – and that certain astrological conditions must pertain. A major shift in the calendar is also essential. This year the moon is in the house of Aries and we are also on the brink of a new century and ready to slough off the skin of the old one to welcome a new age. One other element is required: the ideal host for the Devil's spirit.'

'Blackwood himself, presumably.'

Mycroft shook his head. 'No, the man is too old and frail to withstand the rigours of such an experience. The recipient must be strong, of high intellectual attainment and most importantly, be a sceptic whose sensibilities can be conquered and, converted by the invading sprit. An intellectual agnostic, if you like. Do you recognise those qualities?'

The hairs on the back of my head bristled. 'What are you saying?'

'You are the chosen one.'

'Me? Why, that is ridiculous.'

'Not quite. You fit their requirements ideally and I know that you are their chosen host.'

'How do you know?'

'One of our agents has managed to infiltrate their inner circle. His reports made fascinating reading – until his identity was discovered and he was dealt with.'

I shook my head in disbelief. What Mycroft was telling me seemed so fantastic, so removed from reality that I had difficulty in absorbing it. It was alien to all my rational concepts.

'Well,' I said at last, 'they are on a losing wicket. You cannot think for one moment that I would fall in with their plans.'

'Of your own volition, of course not. But they have ways, very subtle ways of persuasion, coercion, even conversion, which we do not know the what of.'

'Hypnotism?'

'That, no doubt, as well as potions and spells.'

'Spells! You mean magic?'

'I am afraid so.'

'You cannot seriously believe in this mumbo jumbo. What we have here is a group of misguided men, corrupted by dreams of power, placing their faith in the dominion of a figure of folklore. Their intentions may be evil and corrupt but their power is illusory.'

'You are wrong, Sherlock. The gospels tell us otherwise. Was not Our Lord tempted by the Devil in the desert? Did he not cast out demons from poor tortured souls? You know as well as I do that evil is a very tangible force. It inherits the minds and spirits of men and overtakes their finer instincts to commit acts of the most terrible nature. Think of Jack the Ripper and your own Professor Moriarty, men who overstepped the bounds of normal humanity to commit crime, to murder for either pleasure or profit. Were they not hosts to an overwhelming evil spirit?'

'I never thought I would witness my brother ascend to the pulpit,' I replied sourly.

'I am fully aware of your agnosticism. You will change your mind I am sure, but for the moment I will cease trying to persuade you. However, there are practical matters to deal with. Their plan is to lure you down to Howden in Devonshire.'

'And how do they intend to do that?'

'Through Watson, of course. He will persuade you of the need for a holiday to refresh your dismal spirits. You have been rather down recently. The clouds seem to have loured about your head for some considerable time.'

Mycroft was right. I had grown morose. Partly it was because the challenge of crime did not seem so attractive as it once had and partly because I was beginning to feel my age. But there was something else which I could not recognise, like some unseen dark shape at the corner of my consciousness. I could not make out what it was but I was aware that it made me feel gloomy. In retrospect, I now wonder whether it was some force conjured up by Blackwood and his coven.

'And the purpose of this interview...?'

'Is to alert you to the facts. To put you on your guard. You are about to be led into new and perilous territory; it is as well that you are aware of the dangers.'

'If I am able to recognise them.'

'Quite.' The word emerged like a gruff sigh.

It all came to pass as Mycroft predicted. Watson returned from his club one day with news of a cottage ideal for a quiet restorative holiday on the Devon coast. He had been vouchsafed details of this wondrous retreat by a fellow at his club. Edric Cawthorne was his name, a new billiard partner who it seemed to me had made it his business to worm his way into Watson's friendship. It amused me to see the good doctor's enthusiasm for this holiday venture. I knew that his keenness was based on his desire to raise my spirits, to return me to my old self. I wasn't sure that was possible, but it warmed my heart to witness the concern and hope in his eyes.

Arrangements were made and in due course we arrived at the cottage. It wasn't very long before strange things began to happen. I discovered a corpse on the beach. It turned out to be the real vicar of Howden. We were visited by his imposter, who called himself the Reverend Simon Dickens, a fellow supposedly new to the post. It was clear to me that he was one of the satanists. No doubt he came along to the cottage to check up on us. Shortly after his visit we discovered strange runic symbols chalked on our door, probably the work of that man Dickens. They bore no resemblance to any symbols I had encountered before. There was no rhythm to their reproduction as there had been in the case of The Dancing Men, a previous investigation of mine. We encountered Bartholomew Blackwood's son Enoch and his daughter Arabella, a strange wayward young woman with a cunning duplicitous nature. They maintained the fallacy that their father was dead and when we were invited back to their house I had hoped to observe signs of his presence there. However, I did not.

It was as we were leaving the village that Arabella chased after us to issue a warning. 'Get away. Leave this area. It is not safe,' she told us with some urgency and then before we had a chance to question her she departed swiftly.

All these disparate elements – the corpse, the fake cleric, the strange drawings, the meeting with the Blackwoods and the urgent warning – seemed to be unsettling incidents, which on the surface had no tangible connection, but I was convinced they were linked. In some way they were meant to unnerve and confuse me. I was neither unnerved nor confused, but I have to confess that their next move did take me by surprise. They kidnapped Watson. And that is when the nightmare really began.

Twenty-Three

From Sherlock Holmes's Journal

That evening, after I discovered that Watson was missing from the cottage, I set off immediately for Howden. When I reached the village, it was shrouded in darkness. Even the old inn showed no signs of life. It was as though the whole place had been deserted by its inhabitants. But there were lights glimmering through the stained-glass windows of the church, like little bloodshot eyes blinking in the gloom. As I neared the lychgate I could hear the faint sound of singing coming from the church: voices muffled and low and tuneless, chanting some unrecognisable dirge.

In my career as a detective there have been several times when I knew that duty and resilience had to hold sway over discretion and sense. And certainly this was one of those occasions. I was fully aware that I was taking a great risk by entering the church, but what was the alternative? To turn around and leave? Certainly not. My friend's life was in danger. I could not fail him and leave him to the mercy of these Devil worshippers.

And so, clasping my revolver firmly, I approached the church door. As I did so the strange chanting ceased as though those inside were anticipating my entry. If that was the case – so be it. I opened the door and stepped inside.

The interior was lit by a series of large black candles and it took me a few moments to adjust to the strange sepulchral lighting. There was a congregation of around fifty people in the pews, all of whom had turned their faces towards me. Faces that were stoical and grim. At the altar stood the Reverend Simon Dickens, dressed as the others were, in some long flowing dark robe.

His shiny face broke into a large beaming smile. 'Welcome, Mr Holmes. I am so glad you could join us,' he said as though he were greeting a friend at a tea party.

'Where is Watson?' I said, moving down the aisle towards him, my pistol aimed at his chest.

'There is no need for weapons here, Mr Holmes. Fear not, your companion is safe and in good hands.'

'Where is he?'

Dickens moved to the side of the altar and pulled back a curtain to reveal a figure slumped in a chair. It was Watson. His eyes were open, but the pupils were dilated and it was clear from his expression that he was not aware of his surroundings or what was happening. He was in a state of trance induced either by drugs or some form of hypnosis.

As I stepped quickly towards him, the whole scene changed. To my surprise, with a roar of fury, the congregation rushed to prevent me. Before I could respond, I was knocked down to the ground and kicked, the gun flying from my grasp. As I fought back, the face of Enoch Blackwood loomed above me.

'Hold him still,' he said, as he held up a hypodermic needle before him, testing the plunger to ensure the contents of the phial were easily released. I was pinned down to the floor by some of the men I recognised from The Dark Man.

'Time for a little sleep,' Blackwood said, kneeling beside me. 'Roll up his sleeve,' he instructed one of the men.

I tried to struggle but the odds were against me. Blackwood pierced the flesh with the needle and injected the drug. Within seconds my vision blurred and my body felt limp. My captors released their hold on me, but now I was unable to move. My whole surroundings began to fade in a shifting purple mist.

When I awoke I suffered brief memory loss. I could not remember any of the circumstances immediately prior to my falling asleep. I was in a dimly lit chamber lying on a large bed and I was alone. Or so I thought. I felt weak and drowsy and when I tried to rouse myself in preparation for moving from the bed I found that I couldn't. I did not have the strength. I lay back, closing my eyes, and drifted back to sleep for a while. The next sensation I felt was a cool hand on my brow. I opened my eyes and saw Arabella leaning over me, her hand caressing my forehead.

'Poor Mr Holmes. Still feeling a little groggy.'

'Water, please,' I managed to croak.

'Of course.' She disappeared into the shadows and returned shortly with a tumbler of cold water. With her help, cradling my head, I drank it all.

'Feeling better now?' she said.

I nodded and once more attempted to rouse myself to get off the bed, and once again my body failed to respond.

'Rest now,' the girl said with all the softness and serenity of a concerned nurse. 'A good sleep will restore your natural faculties. Lie back and sleep.'

It was all I really wanted to do in my weakened and distorted state, and so I surrendered to the needs of my body and slipped once more into unconsciousness.

When I awoke the next time, my nurse had been replaced by her brother, Enoch Blackwood.

'Welcome back,' he said, failing to keep a tone of menace from his voice.

I was not in the mood for banter and knew that it was a pointless pursuit under the current circumstances. I attempted to accumulate some data if it were possible.

'Where am I?'

'You are a guest in my home.'

Had I felt stronger and less fogged of the brain I might have challenged him regarding the term 'guest', but I let the moment pass.

'And where is Watson?'

'How very concerned you are for that fellow.' He gave me an unpleasant smirk. 'He is in an adjoining room, very much in the same state as yourself – but he is unharmed.'

'What do you want from us?'

Blackwood smoothed the covers on the edge of the bed and sat down. 'To the nub of the matter, eh?'

I said nothing and waited.

'You are here to participate in a ceremony that we are planning, one that will change the very nature of things in this world.'

'A black magic ceremony.'

'One that is allied to the dark forces, yes. Those that truly manifest the real power which controls and alters events.'

'The Devil's work.'

Blackwood gave a throaty laugh. 'Exactly.'

'And you think that I will comply with your wishes?'

'Indeed, yes. We have our methods of persuasion. Besides, we also have Doctor Watson.'

'What does that mean?'

'Oh, I think you know. Indeed I'm sure that you know. A man of your supreme intelligence will appreciate the nature of our threat. We can continue no matter what resistance you exhibit to our plans, but it would make our efforts so much easier if you simply went along with them without resistance. That is why we have Watson. He is our bargaining tool. Do as we ask… or he dies.'

I was still groggy from the drug, but this statement electrified my senses and I felt my heart thump loudly within my breast. I knew words were futile. Any kind of riposte filled with bravado or disdain would have been met with a sneer of merriment. I was helpless and they knew it. I fell back on the pillow in silent despair.

'I will let you rest now,' said Blackwood, his eyes shining with satisfaction. 'We can discuss details later when you are stronger. But at least now you know the scope of your situation.'

I slipped back into sleep, one that was filled with strange dreams. I was wandering down long crooked corridors in some old dark house seeking a door. At times I glimpsed the door at the far end of a shimmering passageway, but as I approached it seemed to merge with the shadows and fade away. And then I was toiling over some barren heathland dotted with wild skeletal trees silhouetted against the wide expanse of grey billowing sky. It was raining hard and the wind was lashing the wetness in my face, blurring my vision. At one point I thought I awoke and found someone leaning over the bed, a skeletal face with dark glittering eyes and skin the texture of old parchment bearing down on me. For some unknown reason this ancient visage terrified me and I screwed up my eyes to dislodge the image from my mind. I held them tight for some time and then, when with some trepidation I opened them again, I was once more standing in a long dark crooked corridor with no sign of a door.

When I did eventually wake, I found Arabella sitting by my bed once more. She smiled at me and helped me sit up.

'How do you feel now you have rested?' she asked in a guileless and innocent fashion.

'Better,' I said, almost mechanically. In truth I did feel refreshed and more my old self.

'I expect you would like some breakfast to build up your strength again.'

I nodded. I knew it would have been foolish to reject food at this time. I needed my strength and energy to facilitate my escape.

My escape? The very words prompted a terrible recollection – they had Watson. I could not escape on my own. I could not leave without him. The possibility of us both leaving this place alive seemed like a lost dream.

Arabella left the room but I heard the key turn in the lock as she did so. Obviously I was not to be trusted. While she was away, I threw back the covers and got out of bed. I rubbed my chin and from the thickness of the stubble I was able to deduce that I had been unconscious for at least two days.

The room was windowless and the only exit was the locked door. I knew that it would be pointless to try and break it down; the noise would rouse my captors. The only thing I could do was wait for events to unfold and hope some opportunity would present itself and enable me to reach Watson.

Arabella returned with a tray containing scrambled eggs, toast and coffee. Her brother accompanied her.

'Eat and then we can discuss our arrangements,' he said with a smile. I devoured the breakfast without comment. When I had finished,

Arabella collected the tray and left me alone with Enoch Blackwood.

'Now, down to business,' he said. 'You, Sherlock Holmes, are our chosen one. Your body will house the spirit and power of our Dark Master. You should feel privileged and blessed.'

'Strange that I do not feel so.'

'No doubt you will after our ministrations. With the coming of All Hallows' Eve, we shall perform the darkest of ceremonies known to mankind: the Corpus Diablo. The celestial conditions appropriate for such a ceremony only present themselves in unison every few hundred years. It is something that my father has been working and preparing for most of his life.'

'And the purpose of this ceremony…?'

'Oh, Mr Holmes, I think you know. It is to make flesh the Devil, to allow the Dark One to walk the earth once more and hold sway over all.'

I shuddered not only at these words but at the cool conviction with which they were uttered. A serene beatific smile rested on his calm features and for a brief moment it was as though he were somewhere else. Suddenly, he broke from this strange reverie, the smile broadening. 'And you will be his host, his human form. He will inhabit not only the shell that is Sherlock Holmes but also the mind. We need an agnostic with a brilliant brain to be the receptacle and that privilege is yours.'

'What if I refuse?'

'You will not be able to or indeed want to when the moment comes. With our help you will be fully prepared, but it is important that you are not… how shall we say… difficult or rebellious. Resign yourself to the task. It will be better for all. And I do mean all. For example, Watson's life depends on it.'

I felt my fists tighten at this declaration. How I would have loved to lash out at that smug face before me. However, I have always had the facility to allow my clearer vision and perceptions to master my baser instincts. I knew nothing would be gained at this juncture by abuse, either physical or verbal; nothing, that is, except a kind of simple satisfaction. Certainly my plight and that of Watson would not be served by such flourishes. I knew I had, in the time-honoured phrase, to keep my powder dry.

What happened in the next few days is confusing and my understanding and memory of them are muddled and fragmented. I was drugged and hypnotised and gradually the rivers of resistance to their plans began to dry up. Indeed, strangely I found myself warming to their ideas and began to feel sanguine about the prospect of being a central part of this most maleficent of ceremonies. Desperately I tried to keep one corner of my mind sane – clear of their taint. However, I am not sure I quite managed it.

I now cannot be certain how long this indoctrination process lasted, but eventually they left me alone. I was treated like an invalid. I was fed regularly and allowed to exercise in the garden and generally I regained strength and composure. I recorded what I could in this journal: one of the few personal favours they granted me. At this time my mind was something of a blank. I seemed to be at ease with my captors and their plans while retaining only a modicum of concern for the health and safety of Watson. It was as though my mind and personality had been split in two. Never before in my life had I felt like this. And I was conscious that the darker side of this nature was slowly but irrevocably taking over. They were indeed weaving their magic spells on me through persistent and prolonged indoctrination.

Although I was aware that there were other inhabitants in the house I never saw anyone but Enoch and Arabella. They attended to all my needs and administered the drugs. Arabella had a strange ambivalent attitude towards me. At times she seemed sympathetic to my plight and even raised hopes within my breast that she might become an ally; but at others she seemed almost fanatical about the forthcoming ceremony. It was clear that her mind was unstable and I certainly could place no reliance on her to help me.

And then one night Enoch came to my room with the news that his father wished to see me. I was led by candlelight up a narrow winding staircase into one of the upper rooms: a large attic, in fact. It was here that I met the man who had been called 'the embodiment of evil'. He sat in a wheelchair by a simple bed. The room was bathed in the flickering amber glow of two oil lamps, the shadows floating in slow waves across the rough plaster walls. As a result, Bartholomew's ancient face, wrinkled and seared like ruffled linen, kept slipping in and out of shadows, resembling some grim gargoyle.

I had seen the face before and then I realised that he had appeared to me when I first came to the house. I thought I had dreamed of this strange figure louring over my bed but in fact I had not been dreaming at all. I had witnessed a visitation from this wizened creature. Strangely I did not feel fearful or ill at ease in his presence.

I was told to sit down opposite this aged creature and then Enoch left us alone. For a time no one spoke and then Blackwood the elder nodded his head in a vague recognition of my presence.

'Good evening, Mr Holmes,' he said, the voice emerging like a creaking door from thin lips that hardly moved.

'Good evening,' I replied, believing that by being courteous I would discover more.

'Tomorrow you will return to Baker Street.'

'What?'

'You are ready to return to… how shall I put it? "Normal life". You will live a normal life now you have been prepared for the glorious future. You will return here a few days before All Hallows' Eve.'

I shook my head in some confusion.

Blackwood smiled at my reaction. 'We trust you now. I dislike the word "indoctrinated" but it is the most appropriate in this case. You are safely in our power and we can control all you do and most of what you think. There is no longer any need to keep you prisoner, for wherever you are… you are under our control.'

I believed him and strangely the thought did not disturb me, which, I reasoned, was proof of their power over me.

'And Watson?' I asked at length, trying to get my mind back on to some kind of practical track.

'He will go with you. He will need hospital treatment…' He held up his shaking hand to silence me. 'He is unharmed, merely in a comatose state from which he will emerge in due course. He will require some time in hospital but apart from partial memory loss he will, in time, be fine.'

'Memory loss?'

'We have removed from his consciousness what has happened to him since he arrived in Howden: his days at the cottage and the time he spent with us in our care. There is now a blank there. It is for his sake – and indeed – your own.'

And so it was that we returned to London: I to Baker Street and Watson to hospital. My brain was numb. I felt no emotions whatsoever. I still functioned as an intellectual being on a perfunctory level but I had no real concern for my friend – only on the surface, rather like an actor playing a part; and I had no misgivings about the destiny that was planned for me by Blackwood and company. So powerful was their influence that the fact that I was to be the living mannequin for the Devil's presence on earth did not concern me one jot. I am conscious of this now as I was at the time, but then the thought of the outcome did not disturb me. And yet… and yet somehow I carried part of my old self in one corner of my brain. My true nature survived but it was imprisoned and I had no energy or very strong inclination to help it break free.

After some weeks convalescing Watson recovered his strength and was able to slough off the trappings of his strange malady. He returned to our old rooms and life, it seemed, resumed its old pattern.

But things were different. There was a strange alteration in our relationship. We were distant with each other. He had no detailed recollection of our time in Devonshire and this made him wary and suspicious; equally I carried a terrible secret with me that must at all costs remain hidden. His life depended upon it.

Enoch Blackwood visited me from time to time to reassure me that things were 'proceeding nicely'. I knew these visits were in reality to act as a reminder as to where my loyalties lay. I was also aware that I was being observed most of the time. It is easy for a detective of my experience to realise when one is being shadowed. For the first time in my life, I was the one under the magnifying glass – but my emotions had been tampered with in such a fashion that I did not care.

Twenty-Four

From Dr Watson's Journal

I stared at Holmes in horror. It was quite clear to me that he was now part of this unholy crew. By some foul means, these devils had somehow interfered with his mind and sensibilities so that now he was theirs. Their puppet. I knew therefore that my life was in real danger, but somehow that seemed less important to me than the deep despair I felt at the change in my friend. In all the years I had known him, he had been an intellectual rock, steady, upright, unwavering in his belief in right and justice. Now, dressed in a travesty of a monk's habit, he stood before me as a member of a satanic coven whose hands were stained with the blood of who knew how many innocent souls.

'What do you want of me?' I asked, simply.

'Nothing, my dear Watson,' came Holmes' reply. His voice was gentle and friendly but the eyes were cold and empty. 'It is a pity you took it upon yourself to interfere. If only you had taken my advice. You would have been much better staying in Baker Street.'

'I came to help you.'

'I do not need your help. Learn from your mistakes. Cause no trouble now and you will be released in a few days. Isn't that so, Brother Enoch?'

Enoch Blackwood gave a nod of the head.

'Then,' said Holmes, addressing the two men who held me, 'take him to the room where he was lodged before. Treat him kindly.'

Without a word they dragged me from the chamber and led me upstairs to the small bedroom. Roughly, I was pushed down on the bed and locked in.

A wave of gloom and despair crashed over me as I lay there on the bed. All my efforts had resulted in this; I was a prisoner once more. And what was worse, the man I had come to rescue, to help, to save from the clutches of Blackwood and his nefarious henchmen, was now at one with them. Holmes' words, those that he had used to me in jest on the beach that ocean of time ago, came back to me: 'O what a noble mind is here o'erthrown!'

With stomach-churning clarity I suddenly realised that my friend was now my enemy.

If truth be told, as I contemplated this sorry state, tears pricked my eyes. The man I respected and revered had by some unholy alchemy been converted into an evil being.

I groaned and prayed for the oblivion of sleep – an escape from the futility of my situation. There was now, I knew, nothing I could do. My situation was without hope.

How long I lay in the darkness before sleep finally rescued me from the misery of consciousness, I do not know. But the next thing I knew I was being shaken gently from my slumbers.

'Come on, old fellow,' whispered a voice in the darkness. 'Rouse yourself.'

It took me some time to realise that the voice belonged to Sherlock Holmes.

My body tensed. What now, my mind cried. What further devilry is afoot?

I sat up in bed without a word and stared at the vague silhouette of Holmes before me in the darkness.

'A fine mess you have made of things,' he said.

I aimed a blow at him but missed.

He chuckled gently. 'Always the man of action, even if it is not the most appropriate action. No, Watson, stay your hand. I have little time. I may be trusted by these people, but I am watched also. The situation is too delicate for them to trust me fully.'

I was about to make some scathing remark about 'trust' but thought better of it. 'What on earth is going on? What in God's name are you up to?'

'In God's name, nothing. In the Devil's... certainly.'

'Enough of riddles,' I snapped.

'Indeed. I had hoped to keep you out of all this, my friend. Unknowingly you have been a pawn in their desperate game. They have forced me to go along with their plans on the understanding that if I did not you would be harmed – murdered.'

'Why didn't you tell me all about it?'

'In order to protect you, of course.'

'What have they made you do?'

He raised his eyebrows in a nonchalant fashion as though he were discussing the weather. 'Nothing concrete just yet, but I have agreed to follow their wishes.'

'And what are they?' I snapped.

Holmes paused before replying. 'What I am about to tell you requires a leap of faith on your part, for we wander now in the realms of the unknown, the supernatural.'

'The supernatural... You cannot...'

'Listen carefully. I know that you are a level-headed, logical man with your feet firmly on the ground. It has always been one of your

179

admirable traits, but in the past when we have been investigating a case this narrowness of vision has prevented you seeing the out-of-the ordinary possibilities that circumstances presented. You sometimes found it difficult to accept the improbable, the recherché.'

'Yes, yes…'

Holmes held up his palm to silence me. 'What I am about to say *is* improbable. It is fantastic, but it is the truth. The clear-headed, clear-sighted truth. Bartholomew Blackwood is still alive and he is masterminding this whole operation. In simple terms, he and his followers are planning a ceremony tomorrow night which may change the destiny of the world.'

'Ridiculous,' I said. It was an automatic reaction but a creeping sense of unease robbed my voice of its conviction.

Holmes ignored my response. 'This ceremony, the Corpus Diablo, can only be performed under certain astrological and astral conditions with the full unfettered participation of an agnostic of high intelligence.'

My blood ran cold. So what Arabella Blackwood had told me about the ceremony and Holmes' involvement was the truth.

'Surely such a thing is not possible.'

Holmes narrowed his eyes and paused briefly before replying. 'I am afraid I believe it is. They intend to make the Devil flesh. To allow the most evil spirit to inherit the physical shell of a human being.'

I shook my head in disbelief. The horror of Holmes' statement lay not so much in the sense of the words but in the manner they were expressed: he appeared to really believe what he was saying. I gazed closely at my friend. His features were drawn, his hair askew and those eyes which were usually sharp and focused shifted uneasily in their sockets. This was not the decisive, self-assured and precise fellow of my long acquaintance. It was clear to me that these satanists had played about with his brain in such a fashion by their infernal means that now

Sherlock Holmes was a confused and vacillating individual.

'You cannot allow this to happen,' I said, grasping his arm.

'It seems it is my destiny,' he replied vaguely. 'I have been chosen to be the Devil's agent on earth.'

'But… why you? You are such a good man.'

'A good man who has doubts about a Christian God. The ideal candidate.' He leaned forward, his gaze upon me, but I, who knew his moods and humours more than any man, could not read anything there. He rustled my bed covers as though he were tucking them in.

I shook my head wildly. 'This is madness. It cannot be…'

Holmes grasped both my wrists. 'All I have told you is true.' He spoke now with such gravity and sincerity that his words almost stopped my heart. How could I not believe him? It was obscene madness, but if Sherlock Holmes told me it was true, then it must be.

As the realisation of the dire and desperate consequences of the situation sank in, my mind suddenly became awash with desperate thoughts.

'What are you going to do?' I croaked. 'You cannot go through with this. You must summon up all your energies to fight against their influences. You must escape. Alert the authorities. Do something…'

Holmes shook his head. 'I am helpless. I am in their thrall. They own me now. Destiny has decreed that I have to follow their path.'

'No, no!' I cried. 'This is madness.'

'Certainly. A madness I tried to protect you from, but I underestimated your tenacity. Not for the first time, I suppose.'

I made to rise from the bed, but Holmes forced me back onto the pillow, hands pulling the bedclothes up to my chin. It was a strange, awkward movement which distracted me for a moment.

'You cannot fight it, Watson. It is too late now. They have won.'

As I stared at that strained white face before me in the gloom, it was joined by three other faces, which had emerged from the shadows.

There was Enoch Blackwood and his sister Arabella, and a less familiar, wizened visage which I realised was the fount of all this evil, Bartholomew Blackwood.

I opened my mouth to cry out, but a cloth was placed over it, the pungent fumes of chloroform quickly assailing and dismantling my senses. Within seconds I swooned once more into darkness.

Part Five

Twenty-Five

From Dr Watson's Journal

When I awoke, I was alone once more in the room. The only illumination was a small candle which flickered low on the bedside table, casting erratic shadows around the walls. I waited a few moments until I had sloughed off the remnants of my drugged slumbers and was fully awake before I attempted to pull myself up in the bed. As I did so, I felt some small weight upon my chest as though an object was lodged there. My hands sought it out. As my fingers slipped around the firm handle and I felt the cold smoothness of the barrel, I realised that it was a pistol.

My heart rate increased as I brought the weapon out from beneath the covers. I wasn't dreaming. It was really a gun, the grey metal glimmering in the candlelight. There could only be one explanation as to how it got there. Sherlock Holmes! With incredible sleight of hand he must have secreted it under the bed sheets as he forced me back against the pillow. The strange mixture of excitement, relief and pure joy that this realisation brought to me is almost impossible to explain. The implications of the presence of this weapon were tremendous. It demonstrated clearly that Holmes was still, to some extent, his own man. There must have been some element of performance in his interview with me, probably because he knew he was being observed. He was a fine actor and certainly on this occasion he had completely taken me in. I could not help but grin broadly for despite the desperate situation we were both in, I could see now that there was still a glimmer of hope that the dark tide of this terrible business could turn our way.

This was my first smile in a very long weary month and I cherished it. Of course, I was fully conscious that the odds were stacked heavily against us, but at least I had not lost Holmes. He had not succumbed fully to the seductions and pressures placed upon him by the satanists. Of course, I should have trusted him. This thought brought another, one less sanguine. I should trust him, but could I still? Had I been given a revolver for other purposes than escape and retribution? Was it another cunning and arcane convolution in their evil machinations?

Slowly my smile faded. If I were to be sensible, I knew that I could trust no one. Not even Sherlock Holmes.

I sought out my clothes and dressed as quickly and as quietly as I could. With only half-formed thoughts of what I intended to do, my first concern was to get out of the room. I tried the window and the door. Both, as I expected, were locked.

I needed my gaoler to release me.

Picking up the metal bowl that rested on a small chest of drawers, I banged it hard against the wall. The hollow clanging sound reverberated around the room. I continued banging, the sound building like the discordant cacophony of church bells. At length, I heard the key turn in the lock. Immediately I sprang behind the door, grasping my pistol by the barrel.

The door opened slowly and a figure entered the room. I recognised the man as one of the villagers, now dressed in the rough monk-like garb. He sensed my presence behind him but before he was able to move or utter a sound, I brought the butt of my revolver down hard on the side of his head. His eyes widened in shock and the mouth opened as though to cry out, but before any sound emerged, I hit him again and he slumped silently to the floor.

I dragged the body into the centre of the room and closed the door. It took but a matter of minutes to exchange our clothes. Once garbed in the loose robe, I left the room, locking the door as I did so.

Although glimpses of the dark blue sky I caught through the narrow windows on the landing told me that it was night, I had no idea of the precise time. Had the cursed Corpus Diablo already started? Had it in fact taken place? I shuddered at this final thought and quickly dismissed it.

The house seemed quiet. It may be that, apart from my gaoler, the rest of the inhabitants were in the church, for surely this was where the infernal ceremony would take place. Slowly, with caution, I made my way downstairs. There was neither sound nor stirring from anywhere. I headed for the hallway and to my surprise and delight found that the main door was unlocked. It was with a wondrous sense of relief that I left the accursed house and found myself outside in a sharp October evening. A hoar frost was already forming on the bare branches and my breath emerged in little white clouds like cigarette smoke. I shivered as the cold night air began to chill me, but I had no time for such considerations. I hadn't a moment to lose. I ran down the drive, out onto the narrow lane and headed for the village and the church.

The main street was deserted and no warm lights emanated from any of the dwellings or the public house. The silence was eerie and for a moment I paused, listening and scanning my surroundings. The street and the church were bathed in milky sepulchral moonlight and the whole scene appeared like a living gothic etching. And then suddenly I observed a figure emerge out of the shadows at the far end of the street.

It was just a silhouette in the gloom but I could see that it was dressed in the same kind of monk-like habit as my own. He made his way with swift strides towards the lychgate. With caution, and keeping to the shadows, I ventured closer and saw him enter the church.

I followed and some moments later, with my heart in my mouth, I turned the old ring handle on the church door and pulled it slightly ajar. The porch was empty but I could see beyond into the body of the church that it was crammed full of people – the evil celebrants, all garbed in dark robes. Some kind of dirge was being played on the organ.

I edged my way forward. Luckily all eyes were on the altar so no one observed me as I took a place in an empty pew on the back row. As I did so, Bartholomew Blackwood appeared out of the shadows at the altar. He was in his wheelchair but with an unsteady motion, he rose to his feet and threw his arms into the air with a strange inarticulate cry.

The congregation gave a roar of greeting, some kneeling as though in supplication, others crying out, 'Master, master.'

'Now is the hour,' intoned Blackwood in a thin reedy voice which rose above the tumult. 'Now is the moment. Now is the glorious time we have all longed for.'

A strangled cheer of approbation rose from the assembled throng and then they knelt down. I quickly followed suit as Blackwood moved slowly towards one of two large ebony thrones placed in the centre of the altar. Gripping the back of the throne, so that only his head was visible over the carved tracery, he addressed his disciples. 'You may guess how elated I am this night, this All Hallows' Eve. For years I have dreamed and planned for this special time. Indeed, I can truly state that the promise of this event has kept me alive. With a successful combination of this auspicious satanic sabbat and the Corpus Diablo I am happy to give up my earthly time. At long, long last our master will be returned to us – in the flesh. Once more he will be able to interfere in and control directly the affairs of man. Our followers will rise like locusts in the field and devour all.'

He paused, his face contorted in a rictus grin, saliva seeping from the corner of his ancient mouth. The congregation chanted their approval. At length, Blackwood moved slowly to stand between the two thrones.

'Let the ceremony begin,' he intoned solemnly.

Arabella mounted the altar, carrying with her a large wicker basket. She set it down on the ground and, throwing back the cover, withdrew a white cockerel. Its feet were tethered but its wings flapped furiously and its tiny head swivelled violently, the beady eyes wild with terror, as though the creature knew its fate. Enoch Blackwood stepped forward, a silver chalice in one hand and a dagger in the other. With swift, deft movements, aided by his sister, he slit the cockerel's throat and allowed the blood that flowed profusely from the wound to drain into the chalice. Again the congregation gave a murmur of gleeful approbation.

Enoch passed the chalice to his father who took it in both hands and held it above his head.

'Please accept this meagre sacrifice, oh Lord of Darkness,' he cried, his reedy voice echoing around the rafters. 'It is a small token of our esteem to welcome you into our midst.' He lowered the chalice and drank from it, before passing it to Enoch, who repeated the diabolical procedure. He then handed the vessel to Arabella who, eyes wide with pleasure, drank in her turn. All three now stood before the congregation, faces wreathed with elation, the fresh blood gleaming on their lips.

Suddenly a stiff breeze blew through the church, dousing a number of the black candles, throwing the whole scene before me into a chiaroscuro picture, unnervingly surreal in aspect.

Enoch disappeared behind the altar curtain to return seconds later with Sherlock Holmes. He was dressed in a long white shroud-like garment with a silver pendant around his neck. My heart sank as I saw that his face was void of expression. He appeared to be drugged or in a trance. Enoch led him to one of the thrones and then, dipping his finger into the chalice, smeared my friend's forehead with the cockerel's blood in the sign of an inverted crucifix. Then Arabella took my friend's hand and led him to the throne on the left-hand side of the altar. I was strangely mesmerised by the scenario which was being acted out before me, as though I were watching some gruesome Grand Guignol play. I knew I had to do something soon to stop this foul farrago from going any further but I felt so helpless. What chance had I against this group of fanatical zealots? I had no idea what they intended to do with Holmes but I knew that it would be terrible.

Bartholomew Blackwood addressed his followers once more, this time in some strange tongue I did not know. They fell to the ground with groans of pleasure. I could do nothing but follow their example, but I kept my eye on the altar and particularly on Holmes.

Blackwood now took up an ancient grimoire and began an incantation in this strange language while both his children swung caskets of incense to and fro over each of the thrones, which gushed out in pungent little black clouds. The dreadful ceremony had commenced. The ceremony of satanic resurrection: the Corpus Diablo.

As Blackwood's voice droned on in its high-pitched hypnotic manner, the temperature in the church suddenly dropped and the wind increased, shaking the drapes that hung down from the rafters.

And then suddenly to my horror and amazement I noticed some kind of movement on the empty throne. Something seemed to be shimmering there, like grey dust or a swarm of flies. They were flies! They clustered together and slowly but inexorably they grew in number. The grotesque writhing form began to take on a definite shape.

Blackwood's incantation continued, rising and falling with exultant cadences as the thing on the empty throne grew darker and firmer. It was turning into the outline of a man! Now I could see his bodily shape: the arms, the legs, the head – the disgusting, rippling, iridescent head.

It shifted and moved like a living, breathing creature, composed of these foul buzzing creatures. Great heavens, I thought, it's the Lord of the Flies. This is the Devil.

The very Devil himself.

Never have I been as frightened as I was at that moment. I felt my whole body freeze with fear, while my heart thudded wildly in my chest. Even my brain seemed in danger of shutting down. For a few moments I thought I would faint but somehow I managed to control my errant passions as I continued to gaze on this diabolical transformation.

Slowly the fly-creature seemed to be turning into flesh.

Holmes, who up to this time had been sitting immobile on his throne, slowly turned his head to gaze at the manifestation beside him. And then in an instant, he was on his feet, withdrawing a golden crucifix from the folds of his robes. He approached the fly-creature, bellowing loudly in the same tongue that Blackwood had been using. Holmes' tones were vicious and victorious.

For a moment the fly-creature began to lose form and then it rallied. Holmes took a step closer and held up the crucifix and repeated his incantation. This time the thing before him began to disintegrate. As it did so, Holmes hurled the crucifix at the apparition. It crashed onto the throne and the buzzing fly-creature dissolved into the air.

For a moment there was absolute silence and stillness, as though time had stood still. Everyone was held immobile and mute by what they had just witnessed. Then there was a brilliant blinding flash of light and the whole building began to shake as though it were caught in the throes of an earthquake. With a great cracking sound, the ground buckled under our feet and hangings cascaded down from the walls. Bartholomew Blackwood was thrown from the dais by the blast and lay in a crumpled heap on the stone floor. The empty throne was now in flames, the fierce yellow tongues of fire shooting high towards the rafters.

There was confusion everywhere. By now masonry was crashing down from the roof of the church and the stained-glass windows were shattering from the power of this unseen force, the coloured glass filling the air like confetti. The congregation cried and yelled in panic, while Arabella Blackwood appeared mesmerised by the scene and stood gazing in frozen fascination at the flaming throne. Enoch, however, was advancing on Holmes, the silver dagger in his grasp, still stained with the blood of the cockerel, raised to strike down my friend. At least this was a situation in which I could take some form of action. I rushed forward, pulling out my revolver, and fired. The sound of the shot added to the general cacophony and the bullet ripped into Blackwood's chest. He turned his shocked gaze upon me, his mouth gaping silently as he felt the pain and then observed the blood spurting from his chest. His face twisted in anger. He took a step towards me, uttering a guttural snarl, his arms flailing wildly, but before he could reach me his legs gave way and he crashed to the ground. His body quivered momentarily, folding into a foetal shape before death finally claimed him.

Holmes turned sharply and spied me. 'Quick,' he cried, leaping off the dais and heading in my direction, 'to the door. We must get out of here fast. This place will come tumbling down at any minute.'

I didn't need any further prompting, and taking my friend's arm, we headed for the church door.

'Shoot anyone who attempts to stop us,' he cried.

In truth the satanists were too fully occupied in their own misery to be concerned about us. Some had been trapped by falling rafters while others were writhing on the floor, crying out inarticulately like bewildered children. They seemed incapable of rational action, as though they had lost all reason.

Behind us one of the pillars cracked, shifted and split in half, thundering down, and bringing with it part of the ancient roof. I could tell that it would not be long before the other pillars followed suit. To add to this destruction, the fire had spread to the hangings scattered on the ground and some of the pews were now alight.

As Holmes and I neared the front door of the church, a robed figure emerged from the shadows to bar our way. It was Simon Dickens. He had a gun and fired at Holmes, who with great presence of mind threw himself sideways, successfully dodging the bullet. I returned fire and caught Dickens in the shoulder. I was about to aim again when I found two arms around my neck and a banshee screaming in my ear. Someone pulled me backwards with such force that I lost my balance, my gun slipping from my grasp. As I tumbled to the ground, I caught sight of the face close to mine, the face of my assailant. It was that of Arabella Blackwood.

When I thudded to the floor, with great agility she rolled to the side and then with a cry of triumph leapt upon me, straddling my chest, her fingers digging into my face, just below my eyes. I winced as the skin scraped away and the blood began to flow. Her features were contorted with fury, her eyes full of cruelty and the blood-smeared mouth champing wildly. I tried to heave her off me but such was her mania that she clamped herself to me like a limpet. Sadly, there was only one thing I could do and so, extricating my arm from her grip, I punched her hard in the face. It was the only time in my life that I have offered violence to a woman and I am not proud of my actions, but I am sure I would have lost an eye had I not acted as I did. With a strangled cry, she flew backwards, blood spurting from her nose. Holmes emerged from the shadows and dragged the unconscious girl from me and laid her on the ground. As I got to my feet, I saw the prone figure of Dickens near the church door. Holmes held up a bloody fist. 'Your bullet helped, old boy, but brute force finished him off. Now let's beat our retreat.'

Because of the shuddering movement of the building, the lintel over the church door had shifted, thus jamming it shut, and even with both of us pulling with all our might, we could not budge it. Behind us more destruction was taking place; with a continuing thunderous roar, the church was collapsing in on itself. Most of the roof was now open to the sky. As I glanced back towards the altar, all I could see were great clouds of smoke and flames. Many of the satanists had been trapped or hit by the falling masonry and their cries of terror filtered through a shifting screen of grey and yellow.

'This is our only chance,' cried Holmes, pointing to a small stained-glass window down the side of the church near the door. Snatching up my revolver he began smashing the glass with the butt. Soon he had created an aperture large enough for us to use. I scrambled through and Holmes followed suit. I cannot express how exalted I felt to be outside that cursed place and breathe in the fresh natural air once more.

'We are not safe here. We must get as far away as possible,' cried Holmes, tugging my arm. We fled through the lychgate and into the street. It was only when we had travelled some hundred yards that we stopped and turned to gaze back at the church. It was now a dark ruined shell, illuminated by the raging fire within, which seemed to reach up to the stars.

'It is a cleansing fire,' observed Holmes. 'The Power of Good has triumphed.'

From Dr Watson's Journal

'It seems that your annuities have recently borne rich fruit,' observed Holmes as he languidly toyed with the strings of his violin.

I raised my eyebrows in mild surprise. I had told him nothing about the little windfall that had just come my way through my small investments. Of course, I knew my friend's pleasure in surprising me with the demonstration of his deductive facilities and I was happy to let him indulge in his old habit.

'And how did you reach that conclusion?' I asked, with a practised smile.

Holmes beamed. 'When I see my old friend with a bright new tie pin and smoking one of Bradley's best Havanas, I know that he has been spending beyond his usual means. As you have not recently indulged in placing your wound pension on some losing nag – as is your usual practice – this extra income could only have come from your investments rather than the racecourse.'

I chuckled, and puffed on my cigar in order that I could send a fine smoke ring in the air in recognition of my friend's accuracy. 'Quite correct,' I added. 'I seem to be as transparent as ever.'

'Only to me,' Holmes grinned. 'Only to me.'

This was two months after our terrible ordeal in Howden and only now were we settling down to what I regarded as normal life again. It was difficult to wipe those dark and horrific memories from my mind – even my dreams were filled with the images of that dreadful ceremony and its aftermath.

Holmes had explained to me in detail a few days after what exactly had happened in the church that night and the events that led up to it. We were lunching at Simpson's, deliberately involving ourselves in the mundane everyday world. We thought the hustle and bustle of the restaurant would help to remind us of our old life, as though, strangely, we were fearful that we had lost it.

'When Mycroft charged me with investigating the Blackwood affair, he arranged for me to meet with Professor Martin Scrowcroft of Cambridge University. He is a medieval historian but also an expert on the occult, having translated *Malleus Maleficarum*, the infamous fifteenth-century grimoire which deals with satanism, witchcraft, devil worship and related subjects. He also is a colleague of Professor Julius Krasinski of Prague University, whose work in this field is second to none. Scrowcroft was somewhat reluctant to talk to me at first when I visited his rooms in Cambridge but when I convinced him of the crucial nature of my work and the possibility of the Corpus Diablo being performed, he relented. This ceremony has only been attempted once before, by an Italian magician and his followers in the seventeenth century.'

'What happened?'

'No one knows for sure. It was attempted in the ruins of an ancient monastery in the Tuscan hills. Travellers found the blackened plague-ridden bodies of those involved some weeks later. Scrowcroft explained the delicate nature of the ceremony: there are so many elements that have to be precisely in place in order for it to be successful; time, location, the astral and astrological conditions must all contend.'

'And the key participant…'

Holmes gave me a dark smile and nodded. 'What was valuable and the most important aspect of my meeting with Professor Scrowcroft was the information he gave me regarding the curse.'

'The curse?'

'The incantation which could stop the ceremony, reverse the process and send the Devil back into the darkness.'

I shook my head. Even though I had experienced the power of the supernatural, sitting here in a busy restaurant, surrounded by innocent folk enjoying their dinners, the whole thing once more seemed far-fetched, ridiculous and the stuff of fantasy. It was as though I was in a period of denial. I sensed that a year from now, I would believe that the whole thing had been a dream. And, indeed, perhaps that would be for the best.

Holmes smiled again. He knew what I was thinking and I guessed that he appreciated my feelings. 'Initially I shared your scepticism, Watson. As a man who has built his life on the belief in human logic, it was a great step for me to take, but as I have frequently observed, when you have eliminated the impossible, whatever remains, no matter how improbable, must be the truth.'

'And it was the truth?'

'And *is* the truth. There is definite evil in the world, evil that goes beyond the corruption in the minds of men. Armed with Scrowcroft's incantation I felt I could disarray the satanists' plans, although I did not know what effect it would have. And, of course, there was the added problem of you. If I did not appear to fall in with their plans, your life would not be worth a pin's fee. In truth, with their potions, drugs and hypnotism, I vacillated anyway. I am a man of a strong mind, as you know, but such was their power over me that I wavered, faltered and even at times, I have to admit, agreed with their aims. To be frank, I had not reckoned on the power that they could wield over a person's will.'

'Shocking as that sounds, I suspected as much. I was convinced that you had indeed thrown your lot in with that devil's brood.'

Holmes paused and took a sip of wine, gazing at me closely over the rim of his glass, and it was then, for the first time, that I noticed the slight change in his appearance. Those steely grey eyes that I knew so well had altered a little. They now seemed to have a vibrant amber speck in them that shimmered brightly.

'I hope that I eventually convinced you otherwise,' he said quietly, a gentle smile creasing his mouth.

'Of course. It must have taken great courage to recite that incantation as that foul fly-creature was manifesting itself beside you.'

'The fly-creature... the Devil himself. I believed that my words would render the ceremony null and void, but I had no notion of the catastrophe they would wreak. It was as in weather conditions: when warm air meets cold there is a heavenly disturbance – a storm – and so it was when the strong forces of evil and good came head to head. The wind of God – literally – brought destruction down on the heads of the satanists.'

As he said these words, a violent vivid set of images replaying the scenes in the church flashed into my mind and I felt my features fix into a grimace.

'Cast those thoughts out now, Watson. It is imperative that you forget all about this affair. To brood on it will lead to despair – madness. It is a dark and dangerous episode in our lives that must be buried... deep.'

'Easier said than done,' I ventured sourly.

'You have great stoical reserve. Engage it now, for your own sake. The outside world will never hear of it. Mycroft has arranged for the village and the church, along with the Blackwoods' house, to be razed to the ground so that nothing remains of Howden or its terrible heritage.'

'Can we really be certain that indeed the ceremony failed and the Devil was sent back from whence he came?'

Holmes paused and he pursed his lips. 'If we have learned anything from this affair it is that nothing can be taken for granted. However, all the evidence points to the fact that the ceremony failed.' He chuckled. 'After all, do I look devilish to you?'

'I see no tail and horns,' I said with a tired grin.

'Good. So let us dispose of this dark episode in our lives into that lumber room of forgetfulness, eh?'

'Indeed.' We raised our glasses and both vowed never to mention this affair again to each other or any living soul, although I made a pact with myself to write about it purely for my own peace of mind, an act of catharsis if you like, not to be published in my lifetime, if ever.

And so we returned to Baker Street and resumed our old life. Or did we? It seemed as though we did on the surface but, in my fanciful way, I thought that somehow we were playing the parts of Sherlock Holmes and Dr Watson rather than *being* those men.

Then something happened that threw my world into confusion once more. It was a misty day in February, just over three months since the terrible events at Howden. Holmes had been sitting quietly by the fireside after consuming a light lunch and appeared to be dozing when there seemed to come a strange whistling sound in the street outside. Holmes suddenly sat up erect in his chair, his eyes wild with excitement, the amber fleck glowing even brighter than normal.

He rose abruptly and headed for the coat rack. 'I have to go out,' he said in a monotone.

'Should I come with you? I could use some fresh air.'

'No, no. I need to be alone. I do not expect to be more than an hour or so,' he replied in the same odd manner, as he quickly donned his ulster and hat. Within seconds he had left the room and I heard his hurried tread down our stairs.

I wandered to the window and gazed down just in time to see Holmes appear on the pavement below. He hesitated for a moment and then with determination he crossed the street, heading towards a figure who appeared to be waiting for him on the other side. It was a young woman who, as he drew close to her, genuflected at his approach. Then she bent forward and kissed his hand. With a deft movement she slipped her arm through his and then gazed up at my window so that I could see her face clearly.

It was Arabella Blackwood.

And she was smiling.

About the Author

David Stuart Davies is a renowned expert on the Great Detective. He is the author of two 'Further Adventures' titles, *The Veiled Detective* and *The Scroll of the Dead* for Titan Books, as well as numerous other Sherlock Holmes novels, and the hit plays *Sherlock Holmes: The Last Act* and *Sherlock Holmes: The Death and Life*. He was editor of *Sherlock Holmes: The Detective Magazine*.

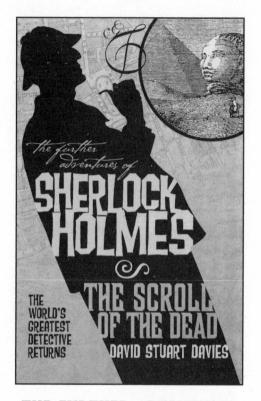

THE FURTHER ADVENTURES
OF SHERLOCK HOLMES
THE SCROLL OF THE DEAD

David Stuart Davies

In this fast-paced adventure, Sherlock Holmes attends a seance to unmask
an impostor posing as a medium. His foe, Sebastian Melmoth is a man hell-
bent on discovering a mysterious Egyptian papyrus that may hold the key to
immortality. It is up to Holmes and Watson to use their deductive skills to stop
him or face disaster.

ISBN: 9781848564930

AVAILABLE NOW!

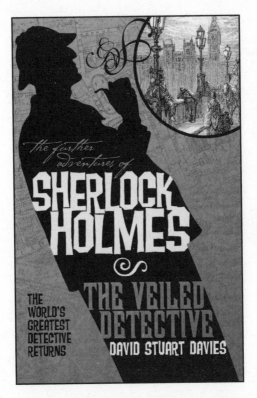

THE FURTHER ADVENTURES
OF SHERLOCK HOLMES

THE VEILED DETECTIVE

David Stuart Davies

It is 1880, and a young Sherlock Holmes arrives in London to pursue a
career as a private detective. He soon attracts the attention of criminal
mastermind Professor James Moriarty, who is driven by his desire to control
this fledgling genius. Enter Dr John H. Watson, soon to make history as
Holmes' famous companion.

ISBN: 9781848564909

AVAILABLE NOW!

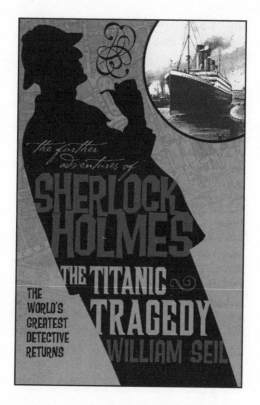

THE FURTHER ADVENTURES
OF SHERLOCK HOLMES

THE TITANIC TRAGEDY

William Seil

Holmes and Watson board the Titanic in 1912, where Holmes is to carry
out a secret government mission. Soon after departure, highly important
submarine plans for the U.S. navy are stolen. Holmes and Watson work
through a list of suspects which includes Colonel James Moriarty, brother to
the late Professor Moriarty—will they find the culprit before tragedy strikes?

ISBN: 9780857687104

AVAILABLE NOW!

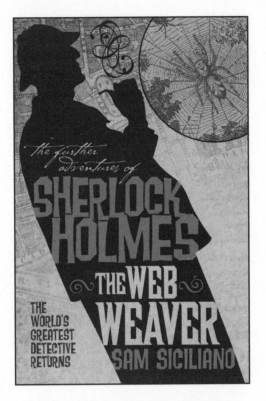

THE FURTHER ADVENTURES
OF SHERLOCK HOLMES

THE WEB WEAVER

Sam Siciliano

A mysterious gypsy places a cruel curse on the guests at a ball. When
a series of terrible misfortunes affects those who attended, Mr. Donald
Wheelwright engages Sherlock Holmes to find out what really happened
that night. Can he save Wheelwright and his beautiful wife Violet from the
devastating curse?

ISBN: 9780857686985

AVAILABLE NOW!

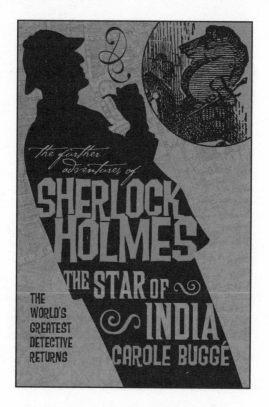

THE FURTHER ADVENTURES
OF SHERLOCK HOLMES
THE STAR OF INDIA

Carole Buggé

Holmes and Watson find themselves caught up in a complex chessboard
of a problem, involving a clandestine love affair and the disappearance of a
priceless sapphire. Professor James Moriarty is back to tease and torment,
leading the duo on a chase through the dark and dangerous back streets of
London and beyond.

ISBN: 9780857681218

AVAILABLE NOW!

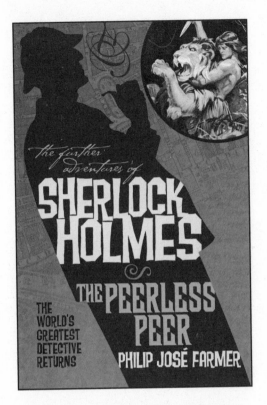

THE FURTHER ADVENTURES
OF SHERLOCK HOLMES

THE PEERLESS PEER

Philip José Farmer

During the Second World War, Mycroft Holmes dispatches his brother,
Sherlock, and Dr. Watson to recover a stolen formula. During their
perilous journey, they are captured by a German zeppelin. Subsequently
forced to abandon ship, the pair parachute into the dark African jungle
where they encounter the lord of the jungle himself…

ISBN: 9780857681201

AVAILABLE NOW!

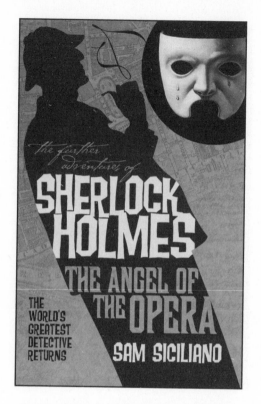

THE FURTHER ADVENTURES
OF SHERLOCK HOLMES

THE ANGEL OF THE OPERA

Sam Siciliano

Paris 1890. Sherlock Holmes is summoned across the English Channel to
the famous Opera House. Once there, he is challenged to discover the true
motivations and secrets of the notorious phantom, who rules its depths with
passion and defiance.

ISBN: 9781848568617

AVAILABLE NOW!

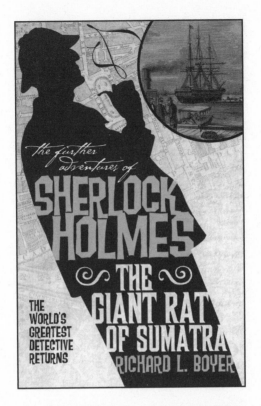

THE FURTHER ADVENTURES
OF SHERLOCK HOLMES

THE GIANT RAT OF SUMATRA

Richard L. Boyer

For many years, Dr. Watson kept the tale of The Giant Rat of Sumatra a secret. However, before he died, he arranged that the strange story of the giant rat should be held in the vaults of a London bank until all the protagonists were dead…

ISBN: 9781848568600

AVAILABLE NOW!

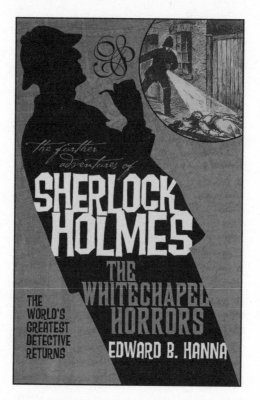

THE FURTHER ADVENTURES
OF SHERLOCK HOLMES

THE WHITECHAPEL HORRORS

Edward B. Hanna

Grotesque murders are being committed on the streets of Whitechapel.
Sherlock Holmes believes he knows the identity of the killer–Jack the
Ripper. But as he delves deeper, Holmes realizes that revealing the
murderer puts much more at stake than just catching a killer…

ISBN: 9781848567498

AVAILABLE NOW!

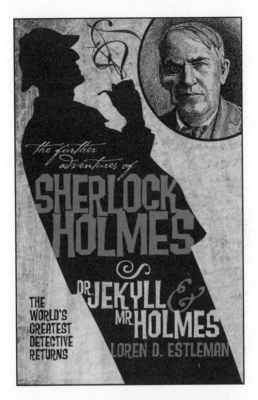

THE FURTHER ADVENTURES
OF SHERLOCK HOLMES

DR. JEKYLL AND MR. HOLMES

Loren D. Estleman

When Sir Danvers Carew is brutally murdered, the Queen herself calls on Sherlock Holmes to investigate. In the course of his enquiries, the esteemed detective is struck by the strange link between the highly respectable Dr. Henry Jekyll and the immoral, debauched Edward Hyde...

ISBN: 9781848567474

AVAILABLE NOW!

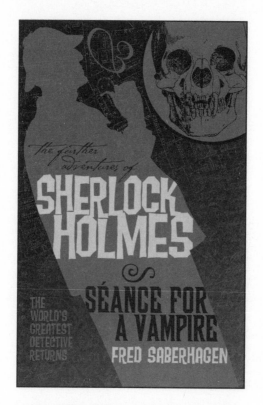

THE FURTHER ADVENTURES
OF SHERLOCK HOLMES

SÉANCE FOR A VAMPIRE

Fred Saberhagen

Wealthy British aristocrat Ambrose Altamont hires Sherlock Holmes to expose
two suspect psychics. During the ensuing séance, Altamont's deceased daughter
reappears as a vampire—and Holmes vanishes. Watson has no choice but to
summon the only one who might be able to help—Holmes' vampire cousin,
Prince Dracula.

ISBN: 9781848566774

AVAILABLE NOW!

THE FURTHER ADVENTURES
OF SHERLOCK HOLMES

THE SEVENTH BULLET

Daniel D. Victor

Sherlock Holmes and Dr. Watson travel to New York City to investigate the
assassination of true-life muckraker and author David Graham Phillips. They
soon find themselves caught in a web of deceit, violence and political intrigue,
which only the great Sherlock Holmes can unravel.

ISBN: 9781848566767

AVAILABLE NOW!

THE FURTHER ADVENTURES
OF SHERLOCK HOLMES

THE STALWART COMPANIONS

H. Paul Jeffers

Written by future President Theodore Roosevelt long before The Great Detective's
first encounter with Dr. Watson, Holmes visits America to solve a most violent and
despicable crime. A crime that was to prove the most taxing of his brilliant career.

ISBN: 9781848565098

AVAILABLE NOW!

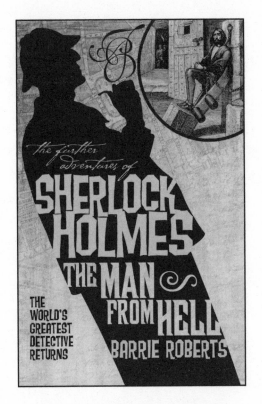

THE FURTHER ADVENTURES
OF SHERLOCK HOLMES

THE MAN FROM HELL

Barrie Roberts

The murder of Lord Blackwater propels Holmes and Watson into an intriguing
case that points to the shadowy figure known only as "The Man from the Gates
of Hell". A tangled web of deceit, violence and tragedy unravels as Holmes'
deductions bring him closer to those behind the plot.

ISBN: 9781848565081

AVAILABLE NOW!

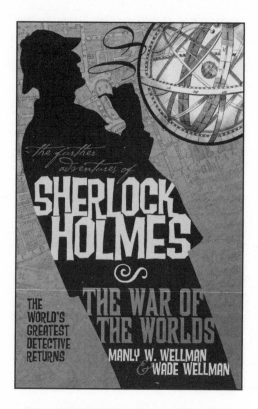

THE FURTHER ADVENTURES
OF SHERLOCK HOLMES
THE WAR OF THE WORLDS

Manly W. Wellman & Wade Wellman

Sherlock Holmes, Professor Challenger and Dr. Watson meet their match when
the streets of London are left decimated by a prolonged alien attack. Who could be
responsible for such destruction? Sherlock Holmes is about to find out...

ISBN: 9781848564916

AVAILABLE NOW!

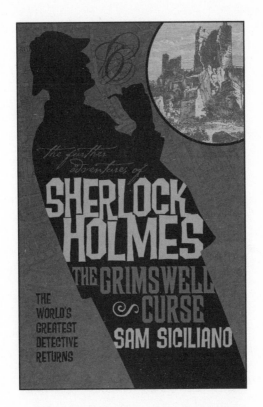

THE FURTHER ADVENTURES
OF SHERLOCK HOLMES

THE GRIMSWELL CURSE

Sam Siciliano

When Rose Grimswell breaks off her engagement to Lord Frederick Digby, the
concerned fiancé calls on Sherlock Holmes, begging him to visit the ancestral home
and discover the reason for her change of heart.

ISBN: 9781781166819

AVAILABLE NOW!

SHERLOCK HOLMES

THE BREATH OF GOD

Guy Adams

A body is found crushed to death in the London snow. There are no footprints anywhere near it, almost as if the man was killed by the air itself. While pursuing the case, Sherlock Holmes and Dr. Watson find themselves traveling to Scotland to meet with the one person they have been told can help: Aleister Crowley.

As dark powers encircle them, Holmes' rationalist beliefs begin to be questioned. The unbelievable and unholy are on their trail as they gather a group of the most accomplished occult minds in the country: Doctor John Silence, the so-called "Psychic Doctor"; supernatural investigator Thomas Carnacki; runic expert and demonologist Julian Karswell... But will they be enough? As the century draws to a close it seems London is ready to fall and the infernal abyss is growing wide enough to swallow us all.

"A rollicking horror-filled adventure featuring the world's greatest detective... This is highly recommended." DREAD CENTRAL

"Smartly written in the familiar Holmes style, the book has a crisp wit, high adventure, knowing nods to literary fans, and a well plotted mystery." THE DAILY ROTATION

"A tremendous amount of fun." HELLNOTES

WWW.TITANBOOKS.COM

SHERLOCK HOLMES

THE ARMY OF DR MOREAU

Guy Adams

Dead bodies are found on the streets of London with wounds that can only be explained as the work of ferocious creatures not native to the city.

Sherlock Holmes is visited by his brother, Mycroft, who is only too aware that the bodies are the calling card of Dr Moreau, a vivisectionist who was working for the British Government, following in the footsteps of Charles Darwin, before his experiments attracted negative attention and the work was halted. Mycroft believes that Moreau's experiments continue and he charges his brother with tracking the rogue scientist down before matters escalate any further.

A brand-new original novel, detailing a thrilling new case for the acclaimed detective Sherlock Holmes.

"Deftly handled… this is a must read for all fans of adventure and fantasy literature." FANTASY BOOK REVIEW

"Well worth a read… Adams is a natural fit for the world of Sherlock Holmes." STARBURST

"Succeeds both as a literary jeu d'esprit and detective story, with a broad streak of irreverent humour." FINANCIAL TIMES

SHERLOCK HOLMES
THE STUFF OF NIGHTMARES

James Lovegrove

A spate of bombings has hit London, causing untold damage and loss of life. Meanwhile a strangely garbed figure has been spied haunting the rooftops and grimy back alleys of the capital.

Sherlock Holmes believes this strange masked man may hold the key to the attacks. He moves with the extraordinary agility of a latter-day Spring-Heeled Jack. He possesses weaponry and armour of unprecedented sophistication. He is known only by the name Baron Cauchemar, and he appears to be a scourge of crime and villainy. But is he all that he seems? Holmes and his faithful companion Dr Watson are about to embark on one of their strangest and most exhilarating adventures yet.

"[A] tremendously accomplished thriller which leaves the reader in no doubt that they are in the hands of a confident and skilful craftsman."
STARBURST

"Dramatic, gripping, exciting and respectful to its source material, I thoroughly enjoyed every surprise and twist as the story unfolded."
FANTASY BOOK REVIEW

"This is delicious stuff, marrying the standard notions of Holmesiana with the kind of imagination we expect from Lovegrove." CRIMETIME

WWW.TITANBOOKS.COM

SHERLOCK HOLMES
GODS OF WAR

James Lovegrove

It is 1913, and Dr Watson is visiting Sherlock Holmes at his retirement cottage near Eastbourne when tragedy strikes: the body of a young man, Patrick Mallinson, is found under the cliffs of Beachy Head.

The dead man's father, a wealthy businessman, engages Holmes to prove that his son committed suicide, the result of a failed love affair with an older woman. Yet the woman in question insists that there is more to Patrick's death. She has seen mysterious symbols drawn on his body, and fears that he was under the influence of a malevolent cult. When an attempt is made on Watson's life, it seems that she may be proved right. The threat of war hangs over England, and there is no telling what sinister forces are at work…

"Lovegrove has once again packed his novel with incident and suspense." FANTASY BOOK REVIEW

"An atmospheric mystery which shows just why Lovegrove has become a force to be reckoned with in genre fiction. More, please." STARBURST

"A very entertaining read with a fast-moving, intriguing plot." THE CONSULTING DETECTIVE